"Roxie, are

Sabrina tentatively moved toward her roommate. "Roxie?" Sabrina could hear her friend softly snoring. Roxie looked far more peaceful than she ever did when she was awake.

Part of Sabrina's mind was telling her to just clean up the glass jar she had just broken in her bedroom and let her roommate sleep, but another more nagging voice kept insisting that something was wrong. Sabrina gave Roxie a little push on the arm, trying to rouse her. "Roxie, it's time to get up."

She's probably just a sound sleeper, Sabrina tried to convince herself, although she knew from personal experience that Roxie had been awakened by lesser noises in the past. Turning back to the window, she gave a point and the blind magically fixed itself while the coins made their way back into the reassembled jar.

"Roxie!" she tried one last yell, but got no response.

Sabrina pushed back the little voice that was quickly growing into a big screaming voice in her mind. Something was definitely wrong.

Sabrina The Teenage Witch®

Where in the World Is Sabrina Spellman?

Sabrina, the Teenage Witch® books

- #1 Sabrina, the Teenage Witch
- #2 Showdown at the Mall
- #3 Good Switch, Bad Switch
- #4 Halloween Havoc
- #5 Santa's Little Helper
- #6 Ben There, Done That
- #7 All You Need Is a Love Spell
- #8 Salem on Trial
- #9 A Dog's Life
- #10 Lotsa Luck
- #11 Prisoner of Cabin 13
- #12 All That Glitters
- #13 Go Fetch!
- #14 Spying Eyes
- #15 Harvest Moon
- #16 Now You See Her, Now You Don't
- #17 Eight Spells a Week *(Super Edition)*
- #18 I'll Zap Manhattan
- #19 Shamrock Shenanigans
- #20 Age of Aquariums
- #21 Prom Time
- #22 Witchopoly
- #23 Bridal Bedlam
- #24 Scarabian Nights
- #25 While the Cat's Away
- #26 Fortune Cookie Fox
- #27 Haunts in the House
- #28 Up, Up, and Away
- #29 Millennium Madness *(Super Edition)*
- #30 Switcheroo
- #31 Mummy Dearest
- #32 Reality Check
- #33 Knock on Wood
- #34 It's a Miserable Life!
- #35 Pirate Pandemonium
- #36 Wake-Up Call
- #37 Witch Way Did She Go?
- #38 Milady's Dragon
- #39 From the Horse's Mouth
- #40 Dream Boat
- #41 Tiger Tale
- #42 The Witch That Launched a Thousand Ships
- #43 Know-It-All
- #44 Topsy-Turvy
- #45 Hounded by Baskervilles
- #46 Off to See the Wizard
- #47 Where in the World Is Sabrina Spellman?

Sabrina Goes to Rome
Sabrina Down Under
Sabrina's Guide to the Universe

Available from Simon & Schuster

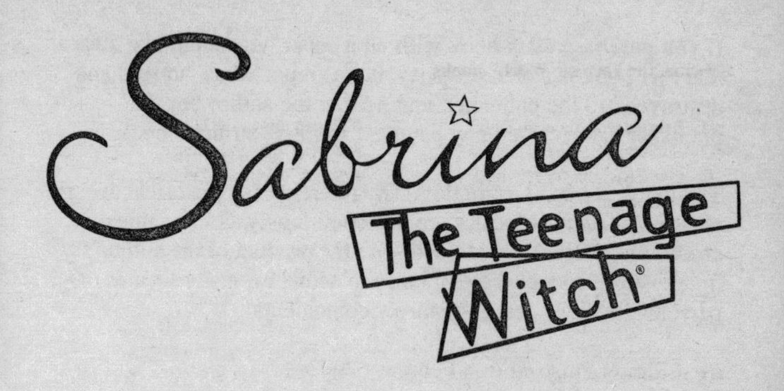

Where in the World Is Sabrina Spellman?

Paul Ruditis

Based upon the characters in Archie Comics

And based upon the television series
Sabrina, The Teenage Witch
Created for television by Nell Scovell
Developed for television by Jonathan Schmock

Simon Pulse
New York London Toronto Sydney Singapore

First Simon Pulse edition February 2003

SIMON PULSE
An imprint of Simon & Schuster Children's Publishing Division
1230 Avenue of the Americas
New York, NY 10020

Printed in the United States of America
10 9 8 7 6 5 4 3 2 1

LCCN 2002105891

ISBN 0-7434-4243-1

For Rachel Battagliese (a.k.a. Mom-mom)—
your many travels have been the inspiration
for this story.

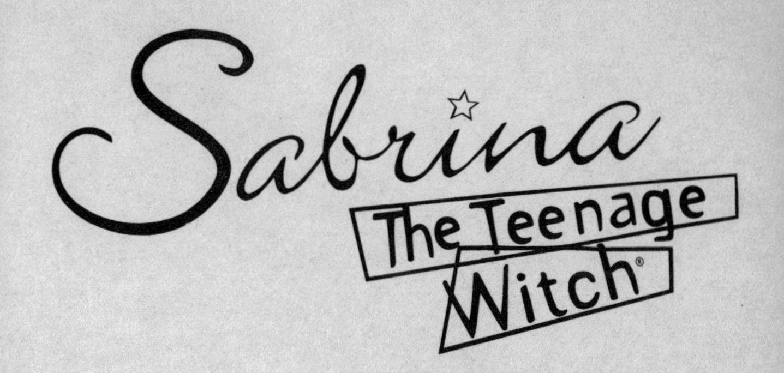

Where in the World Is Sabrina Spellman?

Chapter 1

"What country is bordered by Peru, Bolivia, Brazil, and Argentina?" Salem asked as he read from the notebook lying open on Sabrina's desk. He then began to hum a very annoying tune while waiting for the answer.

"I know this," Sabrina said, searching her brain for the answer. "Don't tell me."

"I really had no intention of doing that," Salem said as he continued humming.

Sabrina let out a little yawn. It was already well after midnight and she wasn't anywhere near finished cramming for her last midterm exam of the week. The World Geography test was scheduled for nine o'clock in the morning, which meant she didn't have any extra time to get up and study before class. She would have to get it all in before bed, which she knew was still hours away considering how badly she was doing on Salem's quiz.

"Colombia!" she excitedly burst out.

"BUZZZZ!!" He made an annoying sound. "The correct answer is Chile."

Sabrina stretched out on her bed and buried her head into the pillow. "That's right! I knew that!"

"Next question," Salem continued, flipping a page with his paw. "What's the only nation that has a Bill of Rights for cows?"

"You've got to be kidding."

"Hey, I'm just reading *your* notes," he reminded her, and continued the irritating humming.

"Well, if it's in my notes, I must have been the one who wrote it down," she said as she made the logical conclusion. "Think, Sabrina, think. . . . Is it India?"

"Ding! Ding! Ding!" Salem cheered. "You are right. Tell the little lady what she's won."

"You know, Salem, I don't think this game show study idea is really helping," Sabrina said.

"Well, if you did what I had originally suggested and gave me a prize every time you got an answer wrong, it would probably be much more fun," Salem noted, "for me, at least. I would be swimming in tuna by now."

"I'm trying." Sabrina yawned.

"And yet, you're still getting most of the questions wrong."

"I'm just too tired," she insisted.

"Well, here's a suggestion," he said. "Stop lying in bed."

Sabrina sat back into her pillows and realized that Salem was right. Studying in bed was not exactly the best idea. "I need some coffee," she said, taking herself off the plush mattress and comforter. "Come on," she said to Salem as she gathered her notebook and laptop computer and went out her bedroom door.

"When are your roommates coming home?" Salem asked cautiously as he followed her into the living room. He usually liked to have some warning before he was forced to go into silent house cat mode.

"Beats me," she replied, depositing her stuff on the coffee table.

"And, more to the point, why aren't they here studying too?"

"Because they already had their last tests and they're out partying," Sabrina said with a sigh. "I'm the only one in the house who still has an exam tomorrow."

"And they all went out without you?" Salem asked as he considered how rude that was.

"That sounds like something I would do."

The front door banged open as Roxie and Miles came in laughing and carrying on like the best of friends. Sabrina considered it a strange sight because Roxie was rarely that cordial to Miles.

"A well-timed question," Sabrina said under her breath to Salem.

"Sabrina, you missed the best party!" Miles said laughing at something that had obviously happened before they had opened the door.

"It was so much fun, even *I* had a good time," Roxie agreed. "It was like the entire school was there."

Sabrina knew that her friend wasn't really a party girl, so for Roxie to have enjoyed herself meant it must have been a party to remember. "Well, *some* people had to be home studying," she said, trying to convince herself that she wasn't the only person on the entire campus who had missed the party. She walked into the kitchen to start brewing a pot of coffee. She still had a long night ahead of her.

"Don't blame us because we got good exam schedules and have a long weekend," Roxie replied as she plopped herself down on the couch.

"You should have stopped by for a little while," Miles said while he joined Sabrina in the kitchen area. "It can't hurt to take a study break."

Sabrina got the coffee grounds out of a cabinet and poured it into the coffeepot. "I don't have the time to take a break. I'm already behind. Besides, I didn't want to be at a party where the theme was to make fun of all the losers who still have tests tomorrow morning."

"That wasn't the party theme," Miles insisted, but Roxie remained quiet as she flipped through the channels on the TV.

The front door swung open once again as Morgan entered with a huge grin on her face. "Wasn't that the best party?!" she asked her fellow party-going roommates. "I'm so glad I'm not one of those losers who still has to take a test tomorrow."

Sabrina pulled a spoon out of the silverware drawer and tried not to slam it shut with frustration.

"Oh, I didn't mean you," Morgan quickly added. "Oh, wait . . . yes I did."

"Thanks, Morgan," Sabrina replied, watching the coffee slowly drip down into the pot. She figured it best to focus on the coffee drip rather than take her frustration out on her roommates. *It's not their fault I had to miss the party to study,* she thought.

"Sabrina, you just have to learn how to schedule your classes better," Morgan replied as she joined Sabrina and Miles in the kitchen. "I always choose the classes I'm going to take *after* I find out the schedules for their midterms and finals. Which is why I only had tests on Monday and Tuesday and got the rest of the week off."

Sabrina looked at Roxie and Miles for support, but the looks on their faces implied that they thought Morgan's opinion was a good idea—at least partially.

"And if all your tests were on the same two days," Sabrina asked, "how in the world did you study for them?"

"I never wait until the last second," she said. "The only cramming I do is when my purchases at the mall don't fit easily into the trunk of the car."

Finally Roxie came to Sabrina's support, "Okay, there is no way that I believe you don't wait until the last minute to study for your tests."

"Listen and learn, girls," she said as she crossed into the living room. "You, too, Miles. You just need to learn the fine art of the study date."

"So you're telling us that you go out with guys just to study?" Miles asked. "No wonder I'm not getting anywhere with girls if that's what they consider a fun date."

"Oh, aren't you cute," Morgan said with a dismissive tone before turning to each of her female roommates. "No. You study *before* the date, then once you and the guy get together, you both realize that you already studied and then go out to dinner instead."

"Then why don't you just agree to go on a regular date in the first place?" Roxie asked.

"Because then you'd have no reason to study all semester," Morgan said, giving them a look like what she was saying was *so* obvious, when in reality this tactic made no sense to anyone but Morgan.

"How can you be sure the guy is going to study before the date?" Sabrina asked.

Morgan rolled her eyes. "It's number seven on the list of rules I give to every guy I go out with," she explained. "How else can I be sure the date is going to go like I want it to?"

Sabrina ignored the fact that her roommate actually gave guys a list of instructions for their dates. "And what if the guy you're going out with doesn't take the same classes you do?" Sabrina asked. "Or he's no longer enrolled in college?"

"Does it hurt to think so much?" Morgan asked, but chose not to wait around for an answer as she hit the stairs. "Well, if I want to oversleep tomorrow morning, I should get to bed now. Good night."

"'Night," the roommates said back in unison.

"Looks like it's that time for me too," Miles said, heading for his bedroom.

Roxie and Sabrina just waved their good nights across the room as they found themselves alone, except for Salem.

"Look Sabrina," Roxie said as she shut off the TV and got off the couch. "It's your own fault for taking so many difficult classes. You always spend so much time stressing out beforehand that you end up cramming for tests at the last minute."

"I like to challenge myself."

"Which is fine, but then you always get like this and start rushing around like crazy. And I don't just mean in school. You're always running around for one reason or another," Roxie said, letting out a yawn. "But at the very last minute you always manage to pull things together and get it done. I'm sure you'll do fine on the test tomorrow."

"Yeah," Sabrina said unenthusiastically.

"Good night," Roxie replied, heading for their room.

"'Night," Sabrina said. She waited for Roxie to shut the door before adding to herself, "I guess she's right. I do work best under pressure."

"Because that's when you usually turn to magic," Salem reminded her.

"I do not."

He just stared blankly at her as if that were enough of a response.

"Most of the time," she quickly added. "But I can't use magic this time. It would be cheating."

"Depends on how you define cheating," Salem said.

"I tend to use the same definition most people do."

"Pity."

"Come on, we've got work to do," she said.

Salem curled up on the couch and closed his eyes. "Actually, I liked your roommates' idea."

"Thanks," Sabrina said, totally not meaning it, as he went to sleep. Although she had to admit that he had helped her out far more than she had expected he would. She must have caught him in an unusually generous mood.

Going back into the kitchen, Sabrina found that the coffee was finished brewing, so she poured herself a cup. She knew it wouldn't be as good as the stuff she served at her aunt's coffeehouse, but the taste wasn't as important to her as the caffeine that was going to help her stay up all night.

Sabrina brought her coffee over to the table and sat down. She opened her notes and started reading about the major exports of the world's largest countries between sips of coffee and a few stray yawns. World Geography wasn't one of her harder courses, but there was a lot of memorization to be done. *And Roxie's right,* Sabrina thought, *it would have been easier if I hadn't waited until the last minute.* But she knew Salem was also right, and the temptation to use magic to help her with the test was beginning to creep into the back of her mind.

The information began to blur together as she read through page after page of notes. Her handwriting, which had been so clear before, was beginning to grow hazy right in front of her. As the night wore on it was getting harder and harder for her to concentrate on the words in front of her. She knew there was very little chance that any of the information was actually sinking into her brain.

Before she knew it, Sabrina was finishing her second cup of coffee and still fighting to keep her eyes open. As she got up to pour a third cup she tried pinching her arm to shock herself awake, but all that did was give her a little red mark.

"This is ridiculous," she said out loud as she put

down the coffeepot without refilling the cup. She looked over to her laptop still sitting on the coffee table in front of the sleeping Salem. *It wouldn't be too hard to boot up my Magic CD-ROM and find a spell to help,* she thought. *No. That would be cheating.*

Sabrina picked up the coffeepot and poured herself some of the steaming hot caffeine. She even spooned in a few extra scoops of sugar, hoping that would also jolt her awake. As she stirred the coffee the movement of the spoon round and round in her cup mesmerized her. Her mind started to drift off into incoherent thought.

"Blech," she said after taking a sip of the horribly sweet concoction. She turned the cup over and spilled its contents down the sink.

"Well, maybe I could just check out one or two spells to help me," she said as she crossed over to the laptop.

Chapter 2

"It's about time," Salem said as she sat beside him on the couch.

"I thought you were asleep."

"Who can sleep when there's the possibility of ill-advised magic in the air?" Salem replied conspiratorially. "So, are we going to give you all the knowledge that's in your textbook? Magically create a copy of the test? Take a trip inside your professor's head?"

"No, Salem. I am not going to cheat," she said as she opened up the laptop. The screen blinked on, and since the Magic CD was conveniently already loaded inside, it started booting up on its own. "I'm just going to find a spell to help me stay up tonight so I can study."

"Well, that's no fun."

Sabrina shot the cat a dirty look. "Sorry my situation is not entertaining enough for you."

"There's always hope," he replied. "I'll hold off final judgment on the entertainment value of this evening until we see how the spell turns out."

Sabrina typed the letters "S-l-e-e-p" into the search window, and the menu jumped through the alphabetical listing of spells.

"Let's see," Sabrina said, reading off the list. "Sleeping Beauty, sleeping potions, sleeping spells . . . no, that's not right."

"Hey, go back to Sleeping Beauty," Salem said. "She stood me up on a date a few hundred years ago . . . said she needed to take a nap."

"Let's try cross-referencing." Sabrina ignored him as she typed in an additional request. "Here we are, 'Sleep, Avoidance of.'" She moved the cursor to the listing and double-clicked it on. The screen flipped to the spell. "It says to enact the Avoidance of Sleep spell, place computer in sleep mode."

"That makes sense," Salem sarcastically chimed in. "This really couldn't get any more boring. Are you sure you don't want to take a little tiptoe through your professor's mind? If you can't find anything on the test, I'm sure there's got to be something you can use to blackmail him into giving you a good grade."

"I'm surprised the Witches' Council didn't sentence you to a *thousand* years in the body of a cat," she said. "Keep up the comments, and you're getting a one-way ticket back to my aunts' house," Sabrina said.

Sabrina followed the instructions on the screen and slid the cursor up to the computer's dropdown menu. She double-clicked on SLEEP, but instead of being met with a blank screen as she usually was when she put her computer to sleep, the monitor turned a deep blue, with pinpoints of light that looked like stars. A bolt of light shot out of the screen and landed beside her. She watched as the light morphed into the form of a man.

Sabrina jumped to her feet next to the mysterious stranger. He wasn't much taller than she was, but he certainly was *much* older. The man was dressed in a ratty-looking long brown coat, with matching brown pants that looked like they had been slept in. He had a flowing white beard that reached all the way down to the floor. His body was trembling as he seemed to be overwhelmed with excess energy.

"Hi-I'm-Rip-Van-Winkle-and-I-assume-you-are-looking-for-an-Avoidance-of-Sleep-spell-to-help-you-out-for-the-night," the strange man said at breakneck speed.

"Whoa," Salem said to Sabrina. "And I thought *you'd* had too much caffeine."

Sabrina was still trying to figure out who this man standing in her living room was. "I'm sorry, I didn't quite catch what you said. Do you mind repeating it a little slower?"

"Hi-I'm-Rip-Van-Winkle-and-I-assume-you-are-looking-for-an-Avoidance-of-Sleep-spell-to-help-you-out-for-the-night," the man said again, though he didn't appear to be speaking more slowly.

"Uh," Sabrina said, still unclear about what he had said. "Why don't we start with a simple question? Who are you?"

"Rip-Van-Winkle."

"Okay, got that." She smiled. "You're Rip Van Winkle. Wait, you mean you're the guy from the Washington Irving story who slept for twenty years?"

The old man nodded his head so vigorously that Sabrina was afraid he was going to hurt himself.

"Who better to enact an Avoidance of Sleep spell," Salem said sarcastically.

"Good point," Sabrina said, then looked back to the man. "Okay, I need a spell that will help me stay up all night so I can study for a test I have to take first thing in the morning. Can you help me out with that?"

"Most-certainly-that's-why-I'm-here-I'm-now-an-expert-at-spells-to-keep-the-subject-awake-ever-since-my-unfortunately-long-nap-that-you-have-obviously-already-heard-about," he said, breathing heavily after all the words had escaped his mouth.

Sabrina's head was spinning. She was definitely too tired to deal with this man. "Maybe we should just stick with yes and no questions for the time being. Okay?"

"Yes," Mr. Van Winkle quickly replied.

"Good." Sabrina put together the questions in her head. "Can you help me stay awake for my test?"

"Yes."

"Does the spell require me to do anything crazy to stay awake for the night that could interfere with my studying for the test?"

"No."

"Okay, now here's the most important question." Sabrina braced herself. "Will the spell have any side effects for me?"

"No."

"Are you sure?" Sabrina insisted, having been though this before with her spells. "I'm not going to be plagued by nightmares? Have to explain myself to the sandman? Or not be able to sleep for the rest of my life?"

"No."

"So there are absolutely no negative reactions for the spellcaster on this spell?"

"Yes," Mr. Van Winkle said, looking very sure of himself.

"Cool," she said with a smile. "Would you cast the spell for me?"

Mr. Van Winkle stepped back to give himself some room. He took a deep breath, bracing himself for the long spell.

> *"So-Sabrina-can-still-cram-for-her-test-here's-the-spell-that-will-work-best. A-jolt-of-energy-a-shot-of-powers-make-her-stay-up-for-hours-and-hours."*

He tapped Sabrina on the head, and she felt the jolt of a thousand cups of coffee coursing through her system. The yawns were gone, and her head was immediately cleared of sleep. She now had the ability to focus on her studies.

"What a boring spell," Salem said, yawning, and he curled himself back up on the couch. "Wake me when something—"

Sabrina silenced him with a point of her finger

and sent him back to the Spellman home.

"Sorry about him," she said to Mr. Van Winkle, sounding totally alert. "And thanks. I feel great."

"Not-a-problem," he replied with a bow before he was sucked back into her computer. The starry sky screen disappeared and was replaced by the blank screen she was used to seeing in sleep mode.

Sabrina closed the laptop. "Wow, I've never felt so awake," she said to herself. "I can't believe this spell has no side effects. This is too good to be true."

Sitting at the dining room table, Sabrina's mind was alert and ready to absorb all the information from her notes. Sabrina flipped back to the first page and read through the entire notebook from cover to cover, carefully studying each page. When she was done she quizzed herself on all the information she had read. It was slow going and methodical work, but Sabrina kept at it and studied like she had never studied before.

When the quizzing was done, she snuck into her bedroom, being careful not to wake her roommate, retrieved her geography textbook, and returned to the dining table for more reviewing. She was so focused on her studies that she didn't even notice when the sunlight started peeking through the window or when the hands on the clock turned to indicate that it was nine A.M.

Chapter 3

"Morning, Sabrina," Miles said with a yawn as he came out of his bedroom.

"What are you doing up so early?" she asked, thinking it was way earlier than it actually was. Even after hours of studying her mind was still surprisingly awake and full of geographical information. She had found the perfect spell.

Miles made his way toward the kitchen for some breakfast. "Some of my friends and I are taking a ride out to the country today to check out some rumored sightings."

Sabrina knew he was talking about aliens, and chose not to pursue the conversation even though she was very curious to find out what they expected to find out there in the daytime. She went back to her studies instead.

"Aren't you supposed to be taking your test

now?" Miles asked after checking the clock on the kitchen wall.

"No, it's not until"—then Sabrina finally noticed the clock read twelve minutes past nine—"now!" She bolted out of the seat so quickly that it fell behind her. "I'm late! Why didn't you tell me it was nine o'clock!?"

"I'm sorry," Miles stammered. "I wasn't . . . I didn't . . . wait a minute, I just woke up!"

Sabrina ran into her bedroom and turned on the light so she could grab some clothes out of her dresser. She banged the drawers open and shut as she pulled together her outfit.

"Hey, I'm sleeping here!" Roxie groggily yelled.

"Sorry," Sabrina replied, grabbing pants and a top from the drawer. "I overslept . . . uh . . . overworked. I'm late!" She considerately turned the light back off before closing the door with a loud slam and running into the bathroom.

Miles watched the *Insane Sabrina Morning Show* from the kitchen while he poured himself some cereal.

As soon as the bathroom door shut, Sabrina pointed at herself and magically changed into the outfit she had grabbed. She paused to give herself the witch equivalent of a shower and tooth brushing before stepping back out the door mere moments after she had closed it.

"Wow, you are in a rush," Miles noted as he hadn't even managed to pour the milk yet.

"It's amazing how motivational stress can be," Sabrina replied. Grabbing an outfit and heading into the bathroom had been for Miles's benefit. She knew she couldn't leave for class in her pajamas, but she just couldn't magically change into her clothes in front of him either. "Be back later," she said as she headed for the door.

"What is going on down here?!" Morgan's voice stopped her before she could turn the knob. "Some people are trying to sleep in, you know."

"Late for my test," Sabrina blurted out as she bolted through the now open door.

Sabrina shut the door behind her and turned her head in all directions to make sure no one was walking in front of the house. Once she had determined the coast was clear she gave another point and magically transported herself into the janitor's closet in the hall outside World Geography. She had been in that particular closet many times before as it made more sense to pop up in there instead of a crowded hallway.

Peeking out the closet door, she noted that the hall was empty of students or faculty. *Everyone's probably in class either giving or taking tests,* she thought. Stepping into the hall, she walked to the closed door of World Geography and silently went inside.

As soon as she had come through the doorway, the entire class picked up their heads and turned in her direction. She could feel her face reddening from embarrassment. Sabrina waited for everyone to return their attention to their tests before stepping up to her professor's desk. "Sorry I'm late," she whispered.

"That's okay, Sabrina," Professor Carter whispered back, handing her a test booklet. "Just take a seat and start working. You've already lost fifteen minutes."

"Thanks." She took the test from him, grateful that he had been one of the more understanding professors. She knew of several other members of the faculty who would have just locked the door as soon as the test had begun and given a zero grade to anyone who showed up late.

Sabrina took an empty seat in the back of the classroom. She noticed that the people around her were hunched over their tests with expressions on their faces that made her suspect the test was very difficult. Professor Carter was a relatively nice professor, but that kindness did not extend to his tests. She knew from experience that his tests were harder than most of the other teachers' in the school.

As soon as Sabrina laid the test out in front of her she realized that in her rush to leave the house she had forgotten to bring a pencil. That would have been a problem for any other student in the class, but Sabrina discreetly pointed to her back pocket and withdrew a perfectly sharpened pencil.

Now that she could finally focus on the test, Sabrina flipped the booklet open and read the first question. Placing her pencil to the page, she wrote down the answer without hesitation. Moving on to the next question she was equally happy to discover that she knew the answer. Question after question, Sabrina continued to be amazed by the spell she had found last night. It kept her mind clear with absolutely no side effects. She could have done without the crazy running around back at the house, but that wasn't really the spell's fault. She had just been a little too focused on her studies.

Sabrina breezed through the rest of the test, easily answering question after question. *I'm going to have to remember this spell when we have finals,* she thought. Naturally there were several questions that still managed to stump her because she couldn't remember the answers, but all in all she did far better than she would have if she had fallen asleep in the middle of her studies last night.

She answered the last question and put her pencil down. For the first time since sitting down, she looked up from the exam and noticed that only a few seats were empty, signifying that not many students had managed to finish before her. Even coming in fifteen minutes late Sabrina thought she had done a great job. Of course the speed at which she finished the test was no indication that she was going to get a good grade, but she was confident that she had answered most of the questions correctly.

Sliding the pencil back into her pocket, Sabrina magically returned it to wherever she had conjured it from before moving to the front of the classroom. When she reached the teacher's desk she noticed that Professor Carter's head was tucked down and he was quietly snoring. *Must be pretty boring to proctor an exam,* she thought. *But I plan to do the same thing and go straight to bed when I get home.*

Sabrina quietly placed the test on the pile on the desk without disturbing him. Back out in the hallway, she once again confirmed she was alone before transporting herself home. She popped up safely on the porch and went inside to find Miles asleep on the couch. His cereal bowl, still mostly full, sat out on the coffee table in front of him.

"Looks like somebody didn't quite make it out of the house this morning," she said, approaching him and giving him a little push on the shoulder. "Miles? Miles, get up. Your friends are probably wondering where you are."

No response.

Well, he was out late, she thought. *I guess those aliens will just have to wait.*

Sabrina went into her bedroom, where she found Roxie, also still asleep. Checking the clock she noticed that it was only ten-thirty and figured her roommate still probably had a good hour left before she had to get up. Sabrina looked at her own bed longingly and knew she was ready to join Roxie in slumber land. Because of the Avoidance of Sleep spell she wasn't exactly tired yet, but Sabrina knew that before long she would need to catch up on the lost rest.

Sunlight was streaming through the window, and Sabrina knew she would never get any rest in such a brightly lit room. Trying her best to be quiet, she moved over to pull down the blinds and hopefully bring at least a little darkness to the room. She knew that she would have to be careful since the blinds had come lose recently and had been giving them a problem. Sabrina had meant to fix them, since it only required the twist of a screw, but she'd kept putting it off. She was tempted to give it a little magical fix but thought better of it in case Roxie happened to wake up midpoint.

Grabbing the pull string, Sabrina gave a gentle tug but nothing happened. She looked to her roommate to confirm Roxie was still asleep before giving the string a stronger yank. This time the blinds tore away from the window and came crashing down to the floor smashing the glass jar full of coins Roxie kept on the table beside the window.

"Sorry, Roxie," Sabrina said as her body tensed. She felt guilty, since she had already woken her roommate earlier in the morning during her mad dash for clothes.

Looking over she noticed that Roxie was still sleeping in her bed. Sabrina felt a sense of foreboding since she knew it was impossible to have slept through that loud crash.

"Roxie?" she stepped over the broken glass and tentatively moved toward her roommate. "Roxie?" Sabrina could hear her friend softly snoring. Roxie looked far more peaceful than she ever did when she was awake.

Part of Sabrina's mind was telling her to just clean up the mess and let her roommate sleep, but another more nagging voice kept insisting that something was wrong. Sabrina gave Roxie a little push on the arm, trying to rouse her. "Roxie, it's time to get up."

She's probably just a sound sleeper, Sabrina tried to convince herself, although she knew from personal experience that Roxie had been awakened by lesser noises in the past. Turning back to the window, she gave a point and the blind magically fixed itself while the coins made their way back into the reassembled jar.

"Roxie!" she tried one last yell, but got no response.

Sabrina pushed back the little voice that was quickly growing into a big screaming voice in her mind. Something was definitely wrong, but she knew she couldn't panic. Not yet, at least. Going back out into the living room, she saw Miles still sprawled out on the couch in the same position he had been in when she'd gotten back from the test.

"Miles." She learned in and heard him taking deep, sleeping breaths. She shook him roughly. "Miles, get up!"

Again, she was met with no response.

"No," she said, not wanting to believe what was becoming painfully more obvious. "I checked with Rip Van Winkle before he cast the spell. There were supposed to be no side effects! He promised!"

And yet, two of her roommates were asleep, and she was unable to wake them.

"Morgan!" Sabrina hurried upstairs to check on her third roommate, but didn't quite make it all the way up. Morgan's body was draped over the top few steps. She had fallen asleep right there on the floor.

"That can't be comfortable," Sabrina said as she bent to her friend. "Morgan? Morgan!"

"What?" Morgan asked, with her eyes still closed.

Sabrina was excited that one of her roommates was awake.

"Prada shoes?" Morgan continued to say in an excited voice. "For me!?"

Sabrina's heart sank when she realized that Morgan was just talking in her sleep.

"No. No. No," Sabrina insisted as she went back downstairs. Giving a point back over her shoulder, she magically transported Morgan back to her own bed so she would at least be more comfortable.

Her laptop was still on the coffee table beside Miles's uneaten breakfast. Sabrina crossed in front of the couch and opened up the computer, hoping to find some answers.

"Excuse me," she said as she pushed the unconscious Miles aside and took a seat beside him while the computer booted up.

She was met with the search screen of her Magic CD-ROM. She typed, "Sleep, Avoidance of" into the search field and hit the enter key. Moments later she was met with the instructions. Not bothering to read them since she already knew what they said, she immediately hit the sleep command on the computer. This time, however, she did not see a field of stars. Instead, an image of Rip Van Winkle appeared on the screen. He was lying on a hill with his back leaned up against a tree. Sabrina felt a pang of dread as she noticed that his eyes were closed.

Sabrina could tell that there was a sign around his neck, but could not read what it said. Sliding the cursor over Van Winkle's sign, she double-clicked on it so it would enlarge. As she had hoped, the sign blew up to fill the screen: SLEEPING—DO NOT DISTURB FOR TWENTY YEARS.

"Twenty years!" she yelled, then turned to

reluctantly confirm that Miles was still asleep beside her.

Seconds later the computer went to sleep, and the screen went blank. Sabrina hit a key to reawaken the computer. The Magic CD-ROM search page flashed on again, but as soon as Sabrina started typing in a request for more information, the computer went back to sleep. Again she hit a key to awaken it and yet again the computer blinked on and then right off.

"Great, even the computer's asleep," she said to herself since no one in the house was conscious to hear her. "This is not good."

Chapter 4

"Aunt Zelda! Aunt Hilda! Help!" Sabrina yelled the moment she popped up in her aunts' living room.

"What is it?" Zelda asked, hurrying in from the kitchen.

"I cast a spell and now my roommates won't wake up!" Sabrina said, too concerned for her friends to worry about covering for her mistake. She had learned on many previous occasions that sometimes it was better to ask her aunts for help than try to work to cover up her mistakes, especially when her friends' lives could be at stake.

"What's wrong?" Hilda asked as she ran down the stairs. She was tugging at something in her hair, but Sabrina couldn't make out what it was. "Where's the fire? And are there cute firemen on the way?"

Once Hilda reached her sister and niece, it was clear to Sabrina that the thing in her hair was a brush. She was struggling against it and trying to get it out with very little success. Sabrina and Zelda forgot what they were talking about for a moment to watch the strange sight of Hilda fighting against a hairbrush.

"What?" Hilda asked like she was doing the most normal thing in the world. "I tried that new Medusa shampoo and it's left my hair in total tangles. Will you two stop staring at me and tell me what's going on?"

Zelda gave her sister a stern look. "It appears that Sabrina has been casting wayward spells again."

"What went wrong this time?" Hilda asked matter-of-factly.

"I'll just ignore the fact that you two don't seem to be surprised and I'll focus on the problem," Sabrina said as she pushed past her own hurt feelings. "I cast an Avoidance of Sleep spell last night so I could stay up to study for a test, which I think I did pretty well on," she added, hoping it would make up for the poor choice of spell. "When I got back from the test this morning, none of my roommates would wake up."

"Is that all?" Hilda asked, obviously relieved.

She had given up on the brush for a moment, and it was dangling from her hair. "You popped in here screaming like it was an emergency."

"Hello! My roommates won't wake up!" Sabrina replied without understanding why her aunt was so casual in her response. To her, the situation seemed to fall under the heading of emergency.

"Well, Sabrina, you shouldn't have used your powers to study for a test," Zelda said calmly.

Sabrina didn't think that this was the time for a lecture. "Can we focus on the problem at hand, here?"

"I am," Zelda insisted. "You shouldn't have used your powers. It was cheating."

"No, it wasn't." Sabrina couldn't believe she was getting into this discussion while her roommates were out like a light back at the house. "I studied. I studied harder than I ever have before, in fact."

"But you used your powers to help you study," Zelda said. "And that gave you an unfair advantage over your mortal classmates. If any of them got really tired they had to fall asleep. It's the same thing as cheating."

"Trust me," Hilda added, tugging at the brush once again. She looked like she was about to rip out some hair to get it free. "It's a fine line I've crossed many times."

"But I didn't have time to study," Sabrina insisted.

"Obviously your classmates made the time to study without relying on magic," Zelda said pointedly.

"Wouldn't it be funny if all her classmates were witches," Hilda added, "and they did the same thing as Sabrina. Oww!" She had given herself one vicious tug at the brush, but it stayed locked in her hair.

Zelda glared at her sister.

"Or not," Hilda said as she frantically tugged at the brush. "Sabrina, you did a bad thing."

"And you used a dangerous spell, too," Zelda added, although her attention was diverted by her sister. "Sleep is an important part of our life cycle. You can't just . . . oh, that's enough!" She gave a point, and the brush freed itself from Hilda's hair.

"Wait a minute," Sabrina said. "You just used magic to do something that a mortal would have had to do on her own."

"That's different," Zelda said.

"How?" Sabrina asked. It was more of a challenge than a question.

"First of all," Hilda replied, "I wasn't being graded for my hairstyling techniques when she helped me."

"Good thing," Zelda mumbled. "And it was something Hilda had no control over. You had many options for the proper way to study before you turned to magic. Did you even try any mortal techniques before you cast the spells."

"I drank coffee and pinched myself," Sabrina said, suspecting that was not the answer her aunts wanted to hear.

"I meant something like not waiting until the last minute to study," Zelda replied.

"I got your point," Sabrina said, even though she really wasn't paying attention. She just wanted to know how to reverse whatever it was that had happened to her friends. "Can you tell me what happened with the spell?"

"When you use an Avoidance of Sleep spell, all of your sleepiness is displaced from yourself onto everyone you speak to," Zelda explained like it was common knowledge.

"So I put my roommates to sleep when I spoke to them?" Sabrina asked, thinking back to her sleeping professor. Obviously her roommates weren't the only ones affected by the wayward spell.

"Same thing happens to Zelda all the time," Hilda said as she received another glaring look from her sister.

"But I checked," Sabrina insisted. "I was told there are no side effects for the spellcaster."

"There aren't—for you. The side effects happened to whomever you spoke to," Hilda corrected. "It's a matter of wordplay."

"But obviously it doesn't affect witches," Sabrina said to her still coherent aunts.

"Actually, it does," Zelda contradicted her niece. "But with some people the reaction is immediate, while for others it takes a couple minutes to kick in."

"But don't worry," Hilda said. "There's a totally easy way to reverse it. All it takes is—"

"Just a second, sister dear," Zelda interrupted, covering Hilda's mouth. "Sabrina used a magical shortcut to get her into this mess, I think she needs to work this one out on her own."

"But I have a bunch of errands to run," Hilda whined. "I don't have time to sleep while Sabrina figures it out on her own. It could take all day."

"Hey!" Sabrina was insulted by her aunt's lack of faith in her. Hilda had said it was an easy problem to reverse.

But both her aunts ignored her as they continued to bicker. "Hilda, it's important that Sabrina learn her lesson."

"She looks fairly educated to me."

"Very funny. It's our job to make sure—"

"But, she's in college now—"

"But that doesn't mean . . ." Zelda's knees buckled as she fell asleep.

Sabrina rushed to her aunt's side and grabbed her before she hit the floor. "Aunt Zelda? Are you okay?" She gently laid her aunt down on the carpet since she didn't have the strength to carry her over to the couch.

"She'll be fine," Hilda said with a smile as she stepped over her sister and moved to the couch. "That's the first fight I've won against her in a long time."

"So, you were saying about the spell being easy to reverse?" Sabrina ignored Zelda for a moment, realizing that she didn't have much time.

"Oh, yeah. It's probably one of the easiest spell reversals. . . ." But Hilda dropped onto the couch before she could finish the thought.

"Aunt Hilda?" Sabrina shook her aunt, but got no response. "Well, that figures."

With her Magic CD-ROM stuck in sleep mode as well as her aunts, Sabrina was losing resources by the minute. She briefly considered consulting the Witches' Council, but past history proved that they spent so much time bickering and questioning things that they would be fast asleep before

Sabrina could even tell them the reason she had come. At least she had her old Magic Book upstairs, and there was always Salem, wherever he might be.

Sabrina briefly considered calling out to the cat, but she quickly realized the pointlessness of that endeavor. She needed to find him without actually speaking to him. Then she needed to communicate the problem without using words. And finally they needed to figure out a way to fix things without having so much as one conversation. It was another typical afternoon at the Spellman home.

For once, luck was on Sabrina's side as she easily found the feline sitting on the kitchen counter. He was poking at a tuna can with his claws, apparently trying to paw it open, but succeeding only at peeling off the label.

"Oh, good, you've come to feed me," he said as she entered the room. "Zelda was supposed to open this while I chased a mouse out of the house, but when I got back inside she was gone."

Sabrina was motioning at him frantically. She kept pointing at her mouth.

"What's the matter with you? Cat got your tongue," he said, laughing much louder than his joke truly deserved. "Oh, I should go into stand-up."

Grabbing the cat, Sabrina carried him out of the kitchen.

"Hey, what about my mid-morning snack!?" he cried, trying to get himself down.

Returning to the living room, Sabrina carefully stepped over her aunt Zelda and put him down on the table behind the sofa.

"Well isn't that nice," Salem said as he saw the aunts lying around. "The poor cat is starving, and his primary food-givers decide it's nap time."

Sabrina continued her manic motioning, trying to communicate with Salem without using sleep-inducing words. He just kind of stared at her for a minute. "Charades?" he asked. "I'm wasting away, here and you want to play charades?"

At first Sabrina shook her head "no," but then, realizing it was her best chance of getting through to the cat, she changed direction and nodded "yes."

"Fine," he said. "I was the charade champion of Other Realm University. But after the game, you're going to feed me, okay?"

Sabrina nodded her head again, then held out her hand with four fingers raised.

"Four words," he said.

Then she switched to one finger.

"First word."

Smiling, Sabrina pointed to her eye.

"See," he said, then fired off more suggestions in rapid progression. "View? Vision? Look? *Look at me, I'm Sandra Dee!*"

Sabrina stomped on the floor to signify he was going way off course. She glared at him and continued pointing at her eye.

"What?" he asked defensively. "Too many words?"

She knew what she was going to have to do, but wasn't sure she had the stomach for it. Pointing at her eye one more time, with magical intent she created an exact duplicate of her eyeball and held it out in her palm.

"Ewww!" Salem squealed. "That's disgusting! I don't want to see your eye!"

Sabrina started jumping up and down, pointing at Salem

"What? What?" He thought back to what he had just said. "Eye? Or do you mean *I,* like the letter?"

Again, she pointed at him, beaming as she made the eyeball disappear.

"Okay, first word is 'I,'" he said. "I think, therefore, I am. . . . No that's five words."

Opening her mouth, Sabrina pointed inside.

"Mouth!" he yelled. "I mouth you! Wait, that makes no sense."

Sabrina kept motioning toward her mouth as she pretended to speak to Salem.

"Teeth? Tongue? Talk? Speak?" he guessed.

She pointed at him when he said "talk" and "speak."

"Which one, talk? Or speak?"

Either works fine for me, she thought. Sabrina put up two fingers to indicate that he should go with "speak" because that worked slightly better in the sentence she was creating.

"Okay, 'I speak,'" he said. "How about 'I *speak,* therefore I am?' No, that's still too many words. Give me more."

She pointed at Salem.

"Me? I speak to myself? Well, I do that all the time. It's the only stimulating conversation I get in this place."

Shaking her head, she tried again. This time she conjured up a giant letter U that hung in midair.

"Hey, that's cheating," Salem said. "You can't use letters."

This is getting us nowhere, she thought. Ignoring Salem's comment, she continued to point to the hanging letter.

"U?" he said. "No, *you*! Y-O-U!"

More nodding.

"I speak you . . . something," he replied. "I speak,

you listen? No, that's not right. I never listen."

Sabrina put her hands together and leaned her head in the sleeping position, closing her eyes.

"Sleep!" He got it right on the first try. "I speak, you sleep!"

She was jumping up and down, pointing at him.

"I speak, you sleep? Sabrina, you totally stink at this game. No wonder your aunts fell asleep in the middle of it." Salem was up on all four paws. "You're supposed to actually do some kind of phrase or title or something. *Gone With the Wind* or *Cat on a Hot Tin Roof.* Those are good charade clues. 'I speak, you sleep' isn't even good grammar. Okay, it's my turn. Let me show you—"

"Salem!" she yelled, before she even realized the words were out of her mouth.

Chapter 5

Sabrina covered her mouth with her hands, but it was already too late. She had spoken to Salem, and it would only be moments before he fell asleep as well.

"Hurry up." She scooped him into her arms and started up the stairs. "We don't have much time. The spell I cast backfired."

"Imagine that."

"Now everyone I speak to falls asleep."

"Cool, I could use a nap," he said as they reached her old bedroom.

"Salem, you probably just woke up."

"Technically," he said. "But I'm a cat. We like napping."

Sabrina didn't have time for his twisted logic. "We have to figure out how to reverse the spell.

Do you know anything about Avoidance of Sleep spells?"

"I thought it wasn't supposed to have any side effects."

"Yeah . . . well . . . *surprise,*" she said as she opened up her old Magic Book. She sat at her desk and put Salem down beside the book. "Do you know anything or not?"

"Sorry," he said. "I've never avoided sleep in my life."

"Figures," she said, flipping through the book until she found the section on sleeping spells. She had hoped the spell she was looking for was in there, since her CD-ROM was the upgraded version of the Magic Book. Luckily, it appeared to be an old spell. "Here it is!"

Sabrina skimmed the page, with Salem leaning in to read it as well. It was in tiny print at the very bottom that Sabrina found what she was looking for. Everything in the book, however, told her what she already knew. Luckily, there was an even smaller footnote at very edge of the page. She conjured up a magnifying glass so she could read it:

FOR MORE INFORMATION, PRESS HERE

There was an even smaller arrow underneath the tiny print. Taking a deep breath, Sabrina placed her finger on the spot and pressed down. With a flash, a very handsome young man appeared beside her dressed in regal clothes that looked like something out of a fairy tale.

"Who summoned me?" he asked with a slight accent that Sabrina couldn't place.

"That would be me," she replied tentatively. "I'm Sabrina."

"Ah, fair damsel," he said with a bow. "I am known as Prince Charming, and it would be a pleasure to help you out of your predicament. Has a sleeping spell gone awry? For I have much practice with sleeping spells."

Please tell me the solution is a kiss from this hunk, she thought. "Actually, a Sleep Avoidance spell," she said hopefully.

"Ah, well, that is a horse of a different color, my dear one," he replied.

"Oh, enough with the sweet talk," Salem jumped in, disgusted by the fawning display. "Can you help us or not? We're racing against the clock here."

"Fear not, oh infuriating feline," Prince Charming replied. "I am impervious to the powers of the Sleep Avoidance spell."

"Finally something works in our advantage," Sabrina said. "So, how do I reverse the spell and wake my friends and family?"

"Ah, but that is an arduous task indeed," the prince replied. "One that frequently requires formidable fortitude and focus."

"This guy likes big words," Salem noted. "And the letter F."

Sabrina shot the cat a look that silently told him to keep quiet.

"You must go on a quest," the prince continued.

"A quest?" she asked.

"A quizzing quest."

"Now he's moved on to 'Qs,'" Salem mumbled as jumped off the desk and moved over to the bed.

"Salem!" Sabrina said through gritted teeth.

"Pay no heed to the calamitous kitty," Prince Charming said, taking Sabrina's hand into his. "For there are more pressing needs to which we must attend. You need to prepare a powerful potion made from ingredients collected by hand from around this grand globe."

"What kind of potion?" she asked.

"One that combines the powers of night and day, sleep and wake, peace and—"

"We got the picture," Salem jumped in. "What do we have to do?"

This time, however, Sabrina didn't glare at the cat, because even she was getting frustrated with the prince's ramblings. "Where do we start?"

"Why, right here, of course." Prince Charming let go of her hand and gave a bow. Sparkles shot through the air as two items appeared on the bed beside Salem. He had to jump out of the way so they didn't pop up on top of him.

"Watch it," the cat said.

The prince just smiled as if he had directed the items to purposely land where they did.

Sabrina moved over to the bed and checked out what had appeared. There was a small maroon and gold cloth bag with a drawstring opening. She assumed that was where she would place the items once they were collected. *There must not be too many things to get,* she thought, since the bag was so small. Beside the bag sat an electrical device of some kind that looked like an overgrown version of one of those mini electronic organizers that most of the students at Adams College seemed to have.

"These items will help you on your quest," Prince Charming said.

Salem had already managed to poke his nose into the bag, obviously checking to see if there was anything in it. *Probably looking for food,* Sabrina thought.

"You will put all of the magical items collected into the sack," he explained. "With each item found, you will receive a new clue on the hunt."

Sabrina picked up the bag. "This isn't very big."

"It is large enough to meet your needs," the prince replied.

Good, she thought. *This will be easy.*

"And this?" Sabrina asked as she picked up the electronic device with her free hand.

"That, my dear, is a truly wonderful magical item," he said. "No matter where you are in the world, it uses magic technology to tell you your exact location and how to get where you need to go."

"Like a GPS system," Sabrina said, referring to the map locator system that car manufacturers were installing in all the new vehicles.

"But you already know its name," the prince said, seeming surprised. "Yes, the Going Places spell will help you out in any locale."

"Going Places spell?" she asked, looking to Salem.

"Witches had the technology first," he explained.

"Before you go on your quest," the prince added, "there are a few rules by which you must abide."

"Why am I not surprised?" she asked.

"That I cannot answer," the prince replied as if it had been a serious question.

"No . . . it's just . . ." Sabrina gave up on trying to explain her sarcasm. "You were saying."

"Once you solve a clue"—he took the device from her—"speak your destination into the GPS. You only have three guesses per clue. Be sure that you only speak into the device when you are certain of your answer. If you miss on all three guesses, you will have failed in your quest, and all of the ingredients you previously collected for the potion will disappear. If you are correct in your solution, the GPS will then transport you to the subsequent destination."

"Sounds easy enough," Sabrina said, not wanting to ask the obvious question. "But, what happens if I fail the quest? What about my sleeping friends?"

"Then you have to start again at the beginning," the prince replied. "The quest will not truly end until the spell is reversed."

Sabrina did not like the sound of that. With a renewed sense of purpose, she went back to the rules. "So I speak into the GPS device and it will take me anywhere in the world?"

"Yes," he confirmed. "However—"

"That figures," she mumbled, knowing that

there was always going to be a "but," "however," "therefore," or any number of words that meant there were more rules to come.

"It will not take you directly to the object," he said. "You must find it on your own. And your magical powers will be limited as well."

"Limited how?" Sabrina asked.

"That I cannot explain," he replied.

"Why not?" Salem asked.

But Sabrina had a more pressing question. "Where is the first clue?"

"It will arrive when you least expect it," he replied. "And now I must be off. Farewell, fair maiden." Taking Sabrina into his arms, he planted a very nice kiss on her lips—the kind that one would totally expect from someone called Prince Charming.

"Wow," was all she could say as he disappeared.

"Earth to Sabrina," Salem said, snapping her back into reality. "Don't you have some spell breaking to do? Not that I'm in any rush to wake up . . . once I fall asleep . . . hey, why haven't I fallen asleep?"

"Beats me," she replied. "My aunts said it takes effect differently on different people, but you really should be out by now. Maybe it's another one of those things where it doesn't affect you because you were with me when the spell was cast."

"Great," he said, without meaning it. "I could have used a nap."

"Well, I could use some help," Sabrina said.

"Hey, you got yourself into this mess."

"At your suggestion," she said, aiming a finger at him threateningly.

"I get your point," he said with a pun. "Where do we start?"

"I guess we wait for the first clue," she replied.

And they waited. But nothing happened.

"Maybe we should check the Magic Book," Salem suggested.

The doorbell rang before they even had a chance to open the book.

Sabrina looked out into the hall. "That sounded like front door, not the linen closet."

"Maybe the clue is being delivered by UPS," Salem suggested.

☆

Chapter 6

☆

"Should we answer it?" Sabrina asked, stepping into the hall.

"I can't think of a better way to figure out who's there," Salem replied as they started down the stairs.

The doorbell rang again, repeatedly, as if the person on the other side of the door was frantic to get into the house.

Sabrina continued cautiously down the steps. "And what if it's just some innocent bystander stopping by? If I say anything, the person will be sent to sleep."

"If it's no one you can talk to, then just slam the door," Salem said. "We've got more important things to do."

The bell rang yet again as Sabrina reached the door. She took a deep breath and opened it to find

Harvey on the other side looking slightly manic.

"Good, you're here," he said, immediately walking inside without being invited. He was speaking almost as quickly as Rip Van Winkle had been the night before. "I just stopped by your house to drop off something for Morgan and when I went inside everyone was asleep and I couldn't wake them. So naturally I figured that something magical was going on, but when I couldn't find you I kind of freaked, so I figured your aunts could help"—he looked into the living room—"except for the fact that they're both asleep right here."

Harvey turned to Sabrina. "So it *is* a witch-related thing. What happened?"

But Sabrina knew she couldn't say anything.

"That's right, Harvey my boy," Salem said, stepping out from behind Sabrina. "Just a little misplaced magic. Don't you miss the days when you were totally oblivious to all this going on?"

"Salem, why isn't Sabrina talking?"

"Well, now, that's the million-dollar question," Salem explained. "See, if she speaks, you sleep. It's just a little spell backfire. Nothing to worry about."

"Is there something I can do to help?" Harvey asked.

"Yes," Salem replied. "I'm starving. Can you open a can of tuna for me?"

Sabrina swatted her hand at the cat intentionally missing him but sending him a message to stop fooling around just the same.

"Okay, fine," Salem said to her. "What should we have Harvey do?"

Sabrina held a finger up to give the universal sign for "hang on a second" to Harvey as she picked up Salem and went into the other room out of earshot from her friend.

"So?" Salem asked once they were a safe distance away in the kitchen.

"Well, we can't take him with us," Sabrina said. "What good is Harvey going to be if he falls asleep the moment we need him?"

"Yeah, but Prince Charming said something about not using your magic," Salem reminded her. "It might help to have an extra pair of hands around."

"How about this," Sabrina said. "We ask him to stay at the house as a backup plan. Maybe I'll be able to use my magic to bring him to us if we run into trouble. Or at least we can give him a phone call here to help if we can't figure out a clue."

"Good idea," Salem said. "And I can keep him company."

"Nice try," she replied. "But I think you'll be more of a help if you come along with me. Someone's going to have to make the call for me."

Sabrina started to head back to the living room, but Salem stopped her. "While we're here, maybe you can help me with this can." He had picked up his unopened snack and looked pleadingly at her.

Not wanting to listen to Salem complain all day about being hungry, Sabrina gave a little point and the can magically opened.

"Oh, thank you, thank you, thank you," he said, sticking his whole face into the tuna and munching away.

Sabrina continued to the living room, where she found Harvey still dutifully waiting for her. He had kindly picked Zelda up off the floor and placed her comfortably in the armchair.

Sabrina pointed to her hand and made a pad of paper and a pen appear so she could let Harvey know the plan without talking to him. However, as soon as reached him, she noticed something very odd: Harvey was standing completely still—like a statue. At first she thought he had fallen asleep standing up, but his eyes were open and she assumed that for him to have managed to remain standing would have been a considerable feat. She moved in closer to Harvey and waved her hand in front of his face hoping to get a reaction, but not expecting the one she received.

"When the hour is close at hands, it's in the tower where Ben stands," Harvey droned on without emotion. "Collect the sound and your first clue's found."

As soon as the last word was out of his mouth, Harvey dropped to the floor.

Sabrina managed to zap a pillow under him to cushion the fall.

"Harvey!" She knelt down and shook him with all her might. He did not respond, of course. He was fast asleep.

Realizing that Harvey was the first clue, Sabrina quickly went to scribble down what he had said, but had a heck of a time trying to remember his words.

"What happened here?" Salem asked, trotting back into the room. "Did you speak—"

"Salem, shush," Sabrina said, trying to get the exact wording down before she forgot it. "Darn!" Too late.

"What happened?" Salem asked, looking over the fallen Harvey. "And why did you put Harvey to sleep?"

"I didn't," Sabrina replied. "When I got back he was in some kind of weird trance. He said something about a guy named Ben and fell asleep. I think it was a clue. Do you know anyone named Ben?"

"Sure," Salem replied. "There's Ben Franklin . . . Ben Kenobi . . . Uncle Ben."

"Salem, be serious," she said, looking over her scribbled notes.

"You're going to need to be more specific."

"It all happened so quickly that I wasn't really paying any attention to what he said."

"Well, we're off to a good start," Salem bitingly replied. "We don't even know the first clue. And it's not like Harvey can say it again."

"Maybe . . . maybe not," Sabrina replied. She pointed to the television, and the screen came on. It showed an image of Salem and her standing in the living room as they appeared right at that moment. "Rewind," she said, and the image started moving backward. On the screen, Salem backwalked out of the room, and Harvey came up off the floor. "Stop. Play."

As Sabrina readied her pen again, the scene she had just experienced played out on the screen.

The image of Harvey on the TV repeated the clue while the real Sabrina wrote it down. "When the hour is close at hands, it's in the tower where Ben stands. Collect the sound and your first clue's found."

"Has he ever considered going into acting?" Salem asked sarcastically. "He's got real presence. A great look for TV."

"Salem, knock it off," Sabrina said, still writing. "Did you get the end of the clue?"

"Nope."

With a frustrated moan, Sabrina played back the scene several times, taking down each missed word carefully. Once she had the full quote she played the scene one last time to make sure she had everything written correctly.

"Can we try a new channel?" Salem asked. "This show's starting to get boring."

Sabrina ignored him. "Okay, so the clue is talking about 'the hour,' so whatever is going to happen is going to happen on the hour."

Salem glanced at the clock. "Well, we've got about twenty-five minutes before noon. Maybe I can have some dessert?"

"Sure," Sabrina said. "If the clue was here in the house we'd have plenty of time for dessert. But, we have to figure out where to go." She brought the page with the clue down to Salem's level. "Harvey specifically said 'close at *hands.*' Like the hands of a clock." Suddenly it all made sense to her. "Like a clock named 'Ben.' The clue refers to Big Ben in England."

Sabrina remembered back to the photo of Big Ben from her geography textbook. The huge clock was in the tower of the British Houses of Parliament. It had four big round faces on each side of the tower that lit up at night. Big Ben was one of the most famous tourist attractions in London, England.

"Technically, I think 'Big Ben' only refers to the bell," Salem corrected her.

"Even better!" She was getting more excited. "The final part says to 'collect the sound and your first clue's found.'"

"How are we going to collect a sound?" Salem asked.

"I'm not sure, but it is a *magical* scavenger hunt," Sabrina said. "So I would assume we're going to be collecting a lot of strange items along the way."

"Okay, I'll buy that," Salem said.

"Let's try the GPS thing and see if we're right," she said excitedly.

As the pair ran upstairs, Sabrina stopped to look back at Harvey, who had fallen at an uncomfortable angle on the floor. Even with the pillow beneath him, she knew he was going to wake up sore—if he ever woke up at all. Since he had been so unknowingly helpful, she decided to make his sleep a little more pleasant with the point of a finger.

Once she and Salem reached her old bedroom, they found Harvey was much more comfortably resting in her bed.

"Didn't we just leave him downstairs?" Salem asked.

Sabrina picked up the sack and the magical Going Places spell device. "Well, here goes nothing," she said, before putting the gadget in front of her mouth. "Take us to Big Ben in Eng—"

Before the last word was even out of her mouth, Sabrina and Salem had disappeared, leaving Harvey behind snoring softly in her bed.

Chapter 7

"—land," Sabrina finished saying as she found herself smack in the middle of a foreign city shortly before sunset. The first thing she noticed was how cold it was standing on the little side street in the fading daylight. Checking around to make sure they were alone, Sabrina zapped up a coat for herself.

London looked exactly as it had in the photos from her textbook. Old stone buildings filled the streets, with a few modern structures scattered about. The fog had rolled in a little and settled low on the streets. Sabrina could still see fairly well, but there was a light haze over everything that just made the place feel even more British to her.

"Are we in England?" Salem asked, looking around. "Where's Big Ben?"

"One question at a time." Sabrina consulted the

GPS and found that the screen had a little map of London on the display. "Yep, we're in England. And the clock doesn't seem to be too far from here."

She could see an arrow with YOU ARE HERE printed next to a little blip on the screen. Another arrow pointed to Big Ben, which appeared to be a few miles—or, more specifically, kilometers—away.

"The clock on this thing says it's four forty," she added. "I guess London's five hours ahead of Westbridge." She then realized the full importance of time. "That means we only have twenty minutes to find the potion ingredient!"

"Better get pointing," Salem suggested.

Sabrina zapped herself and Salem to Big Ben. A moment after she and Salem disappeared, it felt like they bounced off some invisible force field. They suddenly reappeared exactly where they had been standing.

"That was weird," Sabrina said. "Did you feel like . . ."

"Like we hit a wall or something?" Salem finished her question. "Yeah."

"Let's try it again," Sabrina said. She pointed, and the pair disappeared and bounced back again.

"I'm beginning to feel like a Ping-Pong ball,"

Salem noted once they were visible again.

"Prince Charming said my magic would be limited," Sabrina said, remembering back to the rules of her quest.

"But you conjured the coat," Salem reminded her.

Sabrina gave a point and conjured up a matching set of gloves. "This is getting stranger and stranger," she said, thinking over her problem. "Maybe we can't use magic to get us to the ingredient," she suggested.

"Or maybe it's in a no-magic zone," Salem added.

"What's a no-magic zone?" Sabrina asked.

"I think the name pretty much explains itself," Salem replied snidely. "It's a zone where you can't use magic. It would explain the force field we ran into. Take a few steps in the direction of Big Ben."

Sabrina did as she was instructed.

"Now conjure up something," Salem said.

She tried to zap up a hat to go with her outfit. Nothing happened.

"Now come back to me," Salem said. "And try to use your magic again."

Once again, Sabrina did as instructed. This time, the hat appeared.

"It's a no-magic zone," Salem confirmed. "You're not going to be able to use your powers beyond this point. On the bright side, anything you conjure up before you step into the no-magic zone will not disappear when you step into the zone."

"Great," Sabrina said, and she started walking in the direction the GPS was pointing. "And now we only have fifteen minutes!" She didn't like their odds for getting to the clock on time. Conveniently, there was a hotel across the street with a cab sitting at the taxi stand. "We're going to need that cab," she said.

"And how are we going to tell the cab driver where to go?" Salem asked. "Being a talking cat and a nontalking girl won't exactly work for us in this situation."

"You know how you like to pretend to be other people on the phone?" she asked, recalling one of his more annoying habits.

"Yes," he said, smiling and nodding.

"Do you think you could try to do my voice?" she asked.

"Oh, sure. I do it all the time when . . . never mind."

Sabrina made a mental note to pursue the rest of that sentence later. "We'll just have you speak for me," she said as she waved her hand to hail the cab.

The cab started up on the other side of the street. Sabrina began to cross to it, but the driver pulled the car out and swung it around in a wild U-turn, with tires screeching as he came to a stop right in front of her. Sabrina shot a nervous look to Salem as she opened the door and stepped inside the cab.

"Where to?" the cabby asked.

Sabrina loved hearing his British accent.

"Big Ben," Salem said in a high-pitched voice, which sounded nothing like Sabrina's, while she mouthed the words. They really didn't do it as in sync as they had hoped, but it was good enough for the driver, who was looking back at her through the rearview mirror.

"Hold on," he said as the cab lurched to a sudden start, pulling out of the side street and onto a major thoroughfare.

Sabrina immediately regretted stepping into that cab as they practically flew through the streets of London dodging past cars and pedestrians. *On the bright side,* she thought, *we'll get there in plenty of time . . . if we survive.*

Salem slid across the seat as the cab turned a really fast corner. With terror in his eyes, he clawed his way back to Sabrina and jumped into her lap. "Stop the cab," he whispered in her ear. "I'm going to be sick."

"I think this is far enough," she whispered back to him.

Salem got the message. "I think this is far enough," he said to the driver in his bad Sabrina voice.

"Nonsense," the driver replied. "We're almost there."

The cab turned another corner and nearly ran right into a bus.

"Look out!" Sabrina yelled in fear as the cab swerved around the monstrous vehicle. Once again she covered her mouth too late as she realized that they were about to be in even more of a spot of trouble. "We can get out here," she said, trying to convince the driver to stop the cab before he fell asleep. "It's a nice evening to walk."

But the driver did not respond. His head slumped down into his chest as the cab picked up speed.

"Oh dear," Salem said as he buried his head in Sabrina's coat.

The young witch gave a point of her finger, intending to stop the car, but nothing happened. "Nope. My magic's still not working."

"Oh dear," Salem's muffled voice came from her coat.

Sabrina pushed Salem off her lap as she leaned through the window in the plastic barrier that separated the front and backseats. She grabbed on to the steering wheel as the cab careened out of control through the streets while cars dashed out of way. It was hard enough for her to drive on the left side of the road, but nearly impossible to do while leaning in from the backseat.

"Salem, climb up here and hit the brake pedal," she yelled as she tried to bring the speeding car under control.

The cat leaped onto her back and crawled over her. He dropped down to the seat and squeezed his way to the floor between the sleeping cabbie's legs.

"I can't get his foot off the gas," Salem hollered.

Sabrina released the wheel with her right hand and grabbed hold of the cabbie's leg, trying to pull it aside. "Hold on," she screamed as she gave a slight tug on the wheel and she pulled the leg. The cab jolted to the left, and the force of the move and her pulling knocked the leg free.

"Thanks," Salem said as he slowly pressed down on the brake pedal, bringing them to a stop right in front of the Houses of Parliament and Big Ben.

They extricated themselves from the cab as Sabrina considered leaving the driver money for the trip. Then she realized that, aside from the fact that she didn't have any British money, the driver had nearly gotten them killed *before* she had put him to sleep. She left him behind, peacefully sleeping, and looked for a way to get into the clock tower.

The beauty of the clock amazed Sabrina once she got a full view of it. Its face was brightly illuminated and shone through the light fog like a beacon. "Wow," was all should could say.

"Now what?" was all Salem could ask.

She looked at her watch. They still had ten minutes before the clock struck five.

Sabrina noticed that there was a plastic hook on the back of the GPS device, so she hooked it to her belt and then lifted Salem into her arms.

"So how are we going to get inside?" Salem asked. "I don't think they're going to just let us walk right into the tower. And we don't have time for a tour."

"All very good points," she replied, thinking.

"Since the clue said we have to collect the sound of the bell," Salem suggested, "maybe we can just open the bag and get it from here."

"I doubt it would be that easy," Sabrina replied. "And if you're wrong, I don't want to have to wait around England for another hour until it strikes six."

"Which brings me to my original question. How are we going to get inside?"

Sabrina checked out the area. She suspected entering from the front would be difficult to do with a cat in her arms, so she walked toward the back of the building, where she found a pair of guards standing at a gate. "We need to get past those guards," Sabrina said.

"And how are we supposed to do that without the help of your magic?"

"We need a distraction," she replied, placing Salem down on the ground.

"And what do you expect me to do," he asked, "purr at them?"

Sabrina thought about it for a moment, feeling the important seconds ticking away. She looked around the exterior of the building and tried to find a way in that would avoid the guards, but she couldn't see anything. "Wait a second," she said. "We don't need to sneak in."

"We don't?" Salem asked as he watched Sabrina start walking directly to the guards. "What are you doing?"

She just waved him on to follow as she approached the guards. "Excuse me," she said. "I was wondering when visiting hours end."

The guards looked a little confused, considering that someone had walked up to the back gate to inquire about taking a tour.

"The tower's not open to the general public, miss," the more burly looking guard said. "You have to make special arrangements."

"Oh, really." She made a most disappointed-looking face, hoping they would take pity on her instead of just carelessly shoo her away. *Just a bit longer and you'll have a nice nap,* she thought.

"We can give you the number to ring," the other, cuter guard added. "We have it here somewhere."

"Oh, that's awfully sweet of you," she said, adopting the tone of a friendly tourist in need.

"No worry," the cute guard replied.

The more gruff-looking guard just stared at her while the helpful one looked through some papers for the phone number that she knew she was never going to use. She felt a little guilty since she was about to put the guards to sleep while on duty, but she needed to make the potion, and this was the only way to do it. Checking the GPS device on her hip, she saw that there were only minutes until the clock struck five.

"I know I just saw it," the guard said as he continued to look for the number. A moment later, he was asleep.

"David?" the gruff guard was shocked that his partner had just slumped onto the floor. "Get up, chap."

But the guard joined his partner on the ground soon thereafter.

"Let's go," Salem said, plodding past the guards.

Sabrina bent down to grab the keys off the guard before joining Salem at the door to the tower. "Sorry guys," she said back to them.

"They can't hear you," Salem said.

"I know, but I feel bad," she said as she tried different keys in the lock. There were a lot of keys to go through until she finally found the right one. "Let's go!" she said as they burst through the door.

"What about security cameras?" Salem asked as they hit the stairwell.

"No time to worry about them," she said, checking the time yet again. "We've got to move."

Sabrina hit the stairs two at a time, making sure the bag was out and ready to open once she reached the bell. Breathing heavily, she moved up the steps with Salem leading the way.

She eventually came to a door and threw it open to find a huge bell about to start its swing. Sabrina opened the drawstring bag and held it out in front of her, bracing for the loud sound.

GONG!

It rang, and Sabrina could actually see the sound waves as they were magically collected into the bag.

GONG!

"Did you get it?!" Salem screamed over the noise.

GONG!

"I think so!" she yelled back. "But I think we have to collect all the rings!"

"What?!"

Sabrina just nodded her head, trying to cover at least one of her ears with her free hand. The ringing continued for two more tones before Sabrina quickly closed the bag and pulled on the drawstring around the top to keep it secure. She wasn't sure if sound could escape from the bag, but she wasn't going to take that risk. Her ears were still ringing when another guard burst through the door.

"What do you think you're doing?" he asked.

Chapter 8

"We got lost from the tour," Sabrina quickly explained, stepping closer to the guard, wondering if proximity was important in putting him to sleep. "Sorry, but we've been wandering around forever."

But the guard didn't seem to be paying attention. Instead, he appeared to be in the same kind of trance that Harvey had been in when he had given them the clue leading to Big Ben.

"Sabrina, the GPS screen is flashing," Salem said as he nodded to the device hooked onto her belt.

"I wonder what that means," she said, pulling it free.

"For waking times that flow like fountains, more temperate climes are in the mountains," The guard said in a monotone. "Clue two will be seen when you collect the bean." Then he fell to the floor asleep.

"Look, the words came up on the screen." Sabrina showed the instrument to Salem. The device had copied exactly what the guard had said and had printed it out on the display for their review.

"That's convenient," Salem said. "Especially since we don't have a TV around this time. So what's the clue mean?"

"How weird," Sabrina noted, looking at the screen. "I thought the guard said 'climbs' but he said 'climes,' as in climate."

"Thanks for the vocabulary lesson," Salem mumbled. "But what about the clue?"

"Obviously we're looking for a mountain range, but there are mountains with temperate climates all around the world."

"What about the part where he said something about waking times flowing like a fountain?" asked Salem.

"Maybe he meant a liquid that you drink for waking times," Sabrina suggested. "And I can think of nothing better for that than coffee." She looked over the clue. "Yes! It says 'collect the bean,' which must mean coffee bean."

"So we need to go someplace where coffee is grown?" Salem added.

"It makes total sense," Sabrina said. "First we had to collect the sound of a clock's bell, and now we have to get a coffee bean. All the ingredients must have to do with sleep or waking from sleep."

"Well, isn't that interesting," Salem said, not sounding the least bit interested. "But where do we *go?*"

"I've made enough drinks at the coffeehouse to know where the best beans come from." She held the GPS up to her mouth and spoke into its little microphone, "Colombia . . . the Andes Moun"—and in a flash, Sabrina and Salem were transported across the globe—"tains."

When they appeared again, the first thing Sabrina noticed was that the sun was high in the sky again. The second thing she noticed was that they were in some kind of jungle. Checking the time on the GPS screen, she noted that it just after noon, which was around the time that it had been when she and Salem had first left Westbridge.

"It looks like Colombia is in the same time zone as Westbridge," Sabrina said.

"Well, now I know what the clock says," Salem noted. "But what does the map say?"

Sabrina checked the diagram on the screen and noticed that they were deposited a little farther from their destination this time.

"I guess we're trekking through the jungle," Sabrina said, pointing to a path cut through the brush. "And it looks like we've got a bit of a walk, too."

"Oh no," Salem said, shaking his head. "I'm not going anywhere."

"Salem, we have to get the next potion ingredient."

"Need I remind you that I look like a small snack to most of the things that inhabit this place," he said with a shiver. "I'm not moving."

"Fine, you stay here," she said, indicating around her, since they were already in the middle of the jungle. "I'm sure whatever's out there is right *here,* too."

Salem thought for a moment. "You make a valid point. Let's go."

"Wait," she said before he could start down the path. She realized they were probably about to enter another no-magic zone. "Let's try a quick spell before we go."

Salem checked around to make sure nothing was approaching. "Hurry," he said, quivering slightly.

Sabrina gave a point, and a donkey appeared before them.

"Aaacch!" Salem yelled before he realized that

the large animal towering over him was of the harmless variety.

"It's just a donkey," Sabrina said, calming the cat. "Or, more specifically, a burro. I thought he might help us get to whatever coffee plantation we had to get to."

"Good idea," Salem said, breathing heavily as he recovered from the shock.

Sabrina climbed up onto the burro, and Salem hopped up into her lap. "Giddyap!" She gave a gentle kick into the burro's sides.

He didn't move.

"Go!" she said, leaning forward. "Move!"

The burro stood extremely still.

"Maybe he only speaks Spanish?" Salem suggested.

"Great. I took all those years of French in school for nothing," she said, hoping the cat was bilingual. At a few hundred years old he had certainly been around long enough to pick up a couple new languages.

"Don't look at me," Salem replied. "All the Spanish I know would only help us if we were ordering off a menu at a Mexican restaurant."

Sabrina searched her memory for the proper Spanish word. Even though she hadn't learned the language in school, she had heard enough of it on

TV shows and cartoons growing up that she thought she could figure something out.

"*Vamanos?*" she asked skeptically.

The burro took a few tentative steps forward.

"*Vamanos!*" she commanded, and the burro started through the jungle. "Well, that makes sense," she said, referring to the Spanish-speaking burro. "It shouldn't take us too long to get to the coffee plantation."

Sabrina took the reins of the burro and directed it in the direction of the destination blip on the GPS screen.

Salem had apparently underestimated his lack of Spanish knowledge, because he started singing "La Cucaracha" to pass the time as they made their way to the plantation. He was on his third round of the song when Sabrina started to get annoyed with him for making her sit through his singing. It was when he went to start the song for a fourth round that the burro apparently tired of it too.

"Why did we stop?" Sabrina asked.

Salem climbed up the back of the burro's neck and poked his head down into the animal's face. "Looks like we bored the burro to sleep."

"So the spell works on magically created animals too," Sabrina guessed as she stepped down from the burro. As soon as both her feet were on the ground, the animal disappeared. *That's never happened before,* she thought. *Well, at least we're not leaving a defenseless donkey asleep in the jungle.*

"Let's keep moving," Salem suggested as he glanced around for predators.

Sabrina followed as the cat led her up the winding path. The burro had actually taken them a large part of the way before disappearing. However, Sabrina saw on the GPS that they still had a while to go, and on a rather step hill, too.

She was getting much hotter as she walked through the bushes and trees. It didn't take a great leap of logic for Sabrina to realize that the heat probably had something to do with the heavy coat and gloves she still had on. She had gotten so used to wearing the outfit she had pointed up back in England that she had forgotten to take it off. Wishing she could just make it disappear, but having a feeling she might need it later, Sabrina removed the coat and carried it with her.

"Are we there yet?" Salem whined.

"We're getting closer," Sabrina replied, checking to see that their little blip on the GPS screen was getting closer to the other little blip that identified their destination. She felt bad for Salem as he trudged through the brush. Even though they were on a fairly well-cut path, he was having a hard time navigating it since he was built so low to the ground. She thought about carrying him, but she already had her coat in one hand and was using the other hand to clear away branches and bushes that got in her way.

Continuing through the growth, Sabrina kept her eye on the GPS screen to make sure they stayed on the right path. With each footstep she saw that they were getting closer to their destination. The path led to a collection of branches that Sabrina had to push her way through while making sure Salem was close to her. Once they broke through, Sabrina saw a huge coffee plantation with rows and rows of greenery spread out for acres in front on them.

"Wow, talk about a caffeine fix," Salem said, looking over the plantation. "Let's grab a bean and get out of here."

"Wait a second," she said in a whisper as he started for the nearest plant. "We are technically trespassing."

Sabrina looked out and saw some workers on the far side of the plantation. It looked like they were picking the beans. She could also see some men walking the perimeter of the plantation. From where she stood she knew they couldn't see her or Salem because the trees were blocking them.

There was a break in the vegetation between herself and the plantation grounds that was about an acre wide. Sabrina considered just sending Salem out to pick up a coffee bean since he would easily go unnoticed. However, since she had been the one to cast the spell, she wasn't sure whether she had to be the one to collect the ingredients herself to make the reversal potion. The Witches' Council had a tendency to make up tons of rules for even the simplest of tasks, and she didn't want to run the risk that the potion wouldn't work because of a seemingly minor infraction.

Sabrina watched the guards while trying to figure out the best time she could go unnoticed. She would have to make a quick dash while they were turned the other way. Of course, Sabrina knew that she could always put them to sleep if she had to. However, considering all the guards and workers around the plantation, things could be difficult for her in the time it took to knock them out.

"Okay, Salem, here's the plan," she whispered, leaning down to him. Since the plan was little more than running at the right time, it didn't take long to detail.

"Umm . . . I hate to be the one to bring up stupid witch rules," Salem said, looking out over the massive fields of coffee trees. "We can just pick up any bean, right? I mean, we don't have to find one particular bean in all that?"

Sabrina's heart sank a little. It was a question she hadn't even considered, yet it was such an obvious silly little rule the Witches' Council would have devised for the potion to break the spell. And there had to be millions of coffee beans in the field in front of them.

"I don't see how we would know which one," Sabrina said. "The GPS isn't accurate enough to give a reading down to the last bean."

"Okay," Salem said, although there was a considerable amount of doubt in his voice.

As the guards moved off in another direction, Sabrina realized it was now or never. "Let's go," she whispered.

The duo broke out of the trees and ran across the clearing, hoping no one would notice them. It was a short dash, but Sabrina's heart was pounding through the entire run. Once under the cover of the coffee trees, Sabrina let out a sigh of relief. They had managed to go entirely undetected.

BEEP!

The GPS on her belt suddenly came to life

with a noise that was just loud enough to break the silence of the coffee field.

"No!" she whispered excitedly, trying to quiet the device as she grabbed for it.

BEEP!

Sabrina wrapped her coat around the GPS to muffle the sound, but she knew it could still be heard. She turned into the field of coffee trees and started moving away from the perimeter so that she would not be found.

BEEP! BEEP!

"Can't you shut that thing up?" Salem asked.

"I'm trying," Sabrina replied as they moved farther into the trees. "It sounds like it's beeping faster."

BEEP! BEEP! BEEP!

"Maybe we're getting closer to the magic coffee bean?" Salem suggested.

The beeps slowed slightly as they passed an intersection in the rows of tree. Taking a couple steps back, she turned the GPS to the right, but the beeps slowed even more. The sounds sped up again when she turned to the left. Realizing Salem was right and they were searching for one specific coffee bean, Sabrina moved in the direction indicated by the beeping. But that was not the only thing she could hear.

The sounds of footsteps echoed as bodies moved toward her from different directions. The guys who had been watching over the plantation were obviously locked onto the sounds coming from Sabrina and Salem's direction. Not only was the GPS leading Sabrina to the bean, but it was also leading the plantation workers right to her. She tried to cover the sound even more with her coat, but it still escaped and alerted the others to her position.

"There!" Salem yelled, nodding to a tree in front of them

Sabrina followed his gaze as she continued moving forward. Hanging from the tree she saw a glowing coffee bean.

"I guess that's our prize," she said as they reached the bean.

Sabrina was immediately relieved that the beeping stopped. The people running toward her also noticed that the sound had gone, because it no longer sounded like they were coming straight at her.

Sabrina quickly plucked the bean from the tree as she pulled the small bag from her back pocket. Once she opened the bag to deposit the bean, a loud gong from Big Ben escaped. Shocked, she dropped the bean into the bag and pulled the string to close it.

But it was too late. The loud sound had alerted her followers. They were heading back to her position. Five plantation guards burst through the trees and surrounded Sabrina and Salem. The men were blocking any possible route of escape.

☆

Chapter 9

☆

"Um, hi guys," Sabrina said, assuming that they didn't understand English. It didn't really matter. She slowly turned to face each of the guards as she spoke the hopefully sleep-inducing words. "I guess you're wondering what we're doing . . ."

All five of the men were on the ground snoring rather loudly before she even finished her sentence.

"Wow," Sabrina said, shocked that the spell had taken effect so quickly. "I never fully appreciated the power of sleep."

Salem's face lit up suddenly. "Sabrina, I've just had a great idea."

"That's never a good thing."

"With sleep as a weapon," he continued, "you and I could take over the world. And this time, I can't . . . I mean, *we* can't fail!"

Sabrina wasn't surprised that Salem would try to work this situation to his advantage. "Why is it everyone else in the world will fall asleep if I say one word to them, but I'm stuck with you no matter what?"

"Just lucky, I guess," he replied.

Sabrina looked down at the sleeping men. "I thought at least one of them would stay up long enough to give us the next clue," she said with a yawn. "How are we—"

"Over here," Salem said as he walked beside a tree.

Sabrina followed him between the trees and found something entirely unexpected. "That's new," she said as she saw what had drawn Salem's attention.

Coffee beans were on the ground lined up to make letters. Together, the coffee bean letters made a little rhyme that was the next clue on their hunt.

In endless sleep
From mile to mile
The royals keep
A long denial.
Clue three will amass
Within the hourglass.

"I think these things are getting harder," Salem said, looking over the crazy rhyme. "Any ideas?"

"When I think of royals I think of England," Sabrina said. "But we just came from there."

"But that doesn't necessarily mean the spell wouldn't send us right back."

"Maybe it's referring to a part of the world that had kings and queens in the past."

"Well that leaves just about every part of the world," Salem commented. "How about the rest of the clue. Does the hourglass part mean we're going to be time traveling? Or visiting a soap opera?"

"Who knows?" she replied, scanning the area to make sure no one else was coming to check on what had become of the sleeping guards. "Let's think about this. Sand fills an hourglass. *And* it's what the sandman uses to put people to sleep."

"A desert?"

Suddenly, Sabrina's eyes widened. "It's a pun!"

"What?"

"A pun. A play on words."

"I know what a pun is, Sabrina," he replied. "But what are you talking about?"

"The third and fourth lines," she said as she pointed to the collection of words. "They say 'The royals keep a long denial,' like the royalty is denying something for a long time."

"Which is something I've found most kings and queens are prone to do."

"But," she continued, "I think it really means *along the Nile.* It's referring to the Egyptian pyramids where they *keep* the remains of the ancient royalty."

Salem looked at Sabrina. He looked at the coffee bean words. Then he looked back at Sabrina. "What goes on in your head?"

"No, I'm right," she said, standing and pulling the GPS from her belt. "Take us to the Egyptian pyra—"

"—mids," Sabrina finished saying as she and Salem found themselves on the sands of the Egyptian desert. Sabrina assumed they were near the city of Giza, based on the fact that that was the town with the most famous pyramids in the world.

"The world's largest Kitty Litter box," Salem said with awe as he looked out at the miles and miles of sand surrounding them.

Sabrina noticed the vastness of the desert as well, but was more concerned than awestruck. The clue had made a reference to the tombs of the Egyptian leaders, yet she couldn't see the pyramids from where she was standing. Although the sands around them rose and dropped in little slopes and sandbars, she could see far enough into the distance to know they had a long trek through the desert ahead of them.

She looked down at the GPS and saw that the blip that signified her and Salem's position was very far from the blip that signified their target. The time indicated that it was early evening, which concurred with the fact that the sky looked as if the sun had just set. The temperature was comfortable, but Sabrina knew from her studies that the desert could get cold at night. She held tightly to her coat, hoping she wouldn't be there long enough to use it.

"We'd better get moving," she said, but Salem didn't respond. Sabrina looked down at her feet to where she had last seen him, but the cat was gone. "Salem? Salem?" she yelled, searching the area.

"Right here," he yelled back, coming out from behind a little sandbar. "Sorry, I was just . . . enjoying the view."

"We should get going," Sabrina said, looking off across the sands.

"What's the GPS say?"

"You don't want to know," she replied, considering the long distance they had to traverse. A camel appeared at the point of her finger.

"Hey!" Salem yelled as the animal let out a spit in his direction.

Sabrina thought about her conjuring for a moment. She checked the GPS screen again and immediately reevaluated her plan. With another point the camel disappeared, and a two-seated dune buggy took its place.

Salem hopped into the machine. "This is *much* better than a camel!"

"At least I can't put it to sleep," Sabrina replied as she got into the driver's seat. With another point of the finger she magically strapped the GPS device onto the steering wheel in front of her so she could easily glance at it for directions.

Sabrina immediately felt a twinge of concern about driving this strange vehicle through the desert. She wasn't used to driving a stick shift and had never ridden anything on sand before. The convenient thing about being a witch, however, was that all it took was another point of the finger to give herself all the knowledge and skill she would need. Sabrina strapped on her seat belt and turned the key in the ignition, revving the engine.

"Let's roll!" Salem yelled over the roar of the buggy, standing on hind paws to look over the dashboard of the vehicle.

"Just one more thing," Sabrina said, giving a magical ping in his direction.

A cat-size seat belt formed around Salem and pulled him back into the seat. "Awww, you're no fun!"

Sabrina ignored the comment as she put her foot on the gas and tore through the desert. Occasionally glancing to the screen in front of her, she effortlessly changed gears as she crossed the sands. The sky was growing darker, but off in the distance she could begin to see the shadows of three pyramids beyond the rising and falling sands.

"Faster!" Salem yelled over the engine.

"No!" she hollered back. Sabrina was having fun riding up and down the hills, but she knew that going any faster would be dangerous, and they had a mission to complete—preferably in one piece.

The pyramids were getting closer, as well as some other ancient structures that were coming into view. She was trying to see if she could make out Sphinx but figured it was on the other side of the larger pyramids. Sabrina was anxious to see the huge stone statue carved in the body of a lion with a human head. She thought she was almost there when the dune buggy started making a sputtering noise. "What was that?" she asked, looking to the cat.

"How should I know?" he replied. "I haven't driven a full-size vehicle in a very long time."

The buggy began to lurch forward as her speed dropped off in increments. Sabrina pumped the gas pedal and tried shifting gears, but it was no use. The dune buggy slowed to a stop as she realized what the problem was. "We're out of gas," she said, unstrapping herself and Salem from their seats.

"You couldn't conjure up a car with a full tank of gas?!"

"I thought I did," she said in her defense. "Maybe we hit a rock and sprang a leak."

As soon as Sabrina removed the GPS from the steering wheel, the dune buggy dissolved and she found herself falling down into the sand with a bump. Salem landed at her side.

"Pretty convenient that both the burro and buggy disappeared as soon as they became useless," Salem noted.

"At least we're not littering," she commented as she stood and brushed the sand off her. Once she had gotten her footing she started walking in the direction of the pyramids. "It isn't much farther."

Sabrina was a little surprised that they hadn't

run into anybody yet. Granted they were in the middle of the desert, but the Egyptian pyramids were some of the most spectacular tourist sites in the world. *Maybe we're not in tourist season,* she thought hopefully. *Then again, it is pretty late to be touring the desert.*

Checking the GPS it looked like the section of sand she was looking for was on the side of the pyramid where she and Salem stood. She thought it was possible that they could manage to pick up the sand that they needed without running into anyone at all this time.

Plodding through the desert, Sabrina kept slowing down for Salem, who was having a hard time lifting his little legs in and out of the sand. "Come here," she said, bending to him and putting out her arms.

"Thanks," he said as he crawled into her waiting arms and was lifted off the ground.

"We're almost there," she said, balancing the GPS in her free hand, with Salem and her coat in the other. *I should have gotten rid of the coat when I had the chance,* she thought with regret, although the desert breeze was starting to kick up.

It wasn't long before the beeping started again just like it had when they were in the coffee field. This time, with no trees blocking her path,

Sabrina was taken directly to the spot.

A lone camel was circling the area where the beeping led them. Sabrina assumed he must have gotten lost from his owner.

"Why isn't the sand glowing like the coffee bean had been?" Sabrina asked as she bent to the ground and let Salem down.

"Probably because you need a whole scoop of sand," he replied, guessing. "As opposed to the one particular coffee bean."

Sabrina gave a little shrug and pulled the bag out of her pocket. "Stand back. I don't want another of Big Ben's chimes to escape when I open this thing."

Salem did as instructed.

"Hey!" he yelled a moment later.

Sabrina tried not to laugh. Salem had accidentally moved too closely to the camel and had received another near miss from a glob of spit. Sabrina wondered why all the camels seemed to take an instant dislike to Salem.

She bent to the ground, ignoring Salem and the camel. In one flowing motion she quickly opened the bag, scooped up some sand, and pulled the bag shut again, without any sound escaping. "That was easy," she said with a note of satisfaction.

But before she could put the bag in her back

pocket, it started rumbling and shaking violently.

"That doesn't sound good," Salem said, stepping even farther away.

"What's it doing?" Sabrina asked, although she suspected the cat didn't know what was going on any more than she did.

The rumbling grew louder. Before she could do anything, the bag burst open, spitting out all the sand in her face and letting out a gong just to add insult to injury. Sabrina somehow managed to close the bag again even though there was a bunch of sand in her eyes. "But that's where the GPS said to go," she cried while wiping the sand away.

"Maybe we have to dig," Salem suggested as he circled the spot where Sabrina had taken the scoop of sand.

Sabrina double-checked the GPS as she bent beside the cat. They were standing directly on the same spot the screen had indicated they would find their next ingredient for the potion. "It's as good a guess as any," she said with a yawn as she started digging. Sabrina tried to ignore the fact that that was her second yawn in the past several minutes. She figured if she ignored the sleepiness she was beginning to feel, then it might go away.

Luckily the sand was rather loosely packed, so

it wasn't hard for Sabrina to push it away with her hands. She was impressed with Salem's abilities as he joined in. Even though his front paws were much smaller than Sabrina's two hands, he was moving them at such a speed that he was displacing almost the same amount of sand as Sabrina. *Then again,* she thought, *he has had a lot of practice digging through sand.*

Although the sand was easy to move, Sabrina found herself exerting a tremendous amount of energy as the hole got deeper and deeper. The repetitive motion of the digging was beginning to lull her into a hypnotic state. Her digging slowed slightly. She was getting tired.

Luckily, the silence that hung in the air was broken by Salem's yell: "AAAAGGGHHHH!"

"Salem, are you okay?" she asked the cat after he fell into the shallow hole.

Curled up on his back, disproving the notion that cats always land on their feet, he answered with disgust, "Fine."

Salem righted himself, but as his paws brushed away at the sand beneath him, a soft glow emanated through the ground. "I think we've found our ingredient," he said, brushing the rest of it away.

Sabrina leaned into the hole and saw a glowing

patch of sand. She pulled Salem out of the ground and readied the bag once more. Taking a breath, she scooped up the glowing sand much as she had done the first batch, without allowing another sound of Big Ben to escape.

"Got it," she said. Although she had seen the sand go in, the bag felt curiously empty. Neither the coffee bean nor the sand seemed to be inside. *This magic bag certainly makes carrying things around easier.* "Keep an eye out for another clue."

Sabrina and Salem checked around for someone to tell them the next clue, but they were still the only ones out in the desert. They walked around a bit to see if the clue had been written in the sand, but the area was totally smooth. The camel followed them as they searched. Several times he came precariously close to stepping on Salem.

"Watch it, hump boy," Salem said, foolishly threatening the animal that towered over him.

Surprisingly, the camel answered back. "Up where lines converge, is the place you will go; where the white bears emerge with a ho, ho, and ho. To wake with a splash, clue four is your stash."

"The North Pole!" Sabrina and Salem cheered in unison.

The camel gave an apathetic spit and fell asleep standing up.

Salem eyed the beast of burden. "Okay, that was a little freaky."

"Says the talking cat," Sabrina added.

☆

Chapter 10

☆

Sabrina picked up the GPS device and spoke the words "North Pole."

But this time nothing happened.

"Maybe I didn't speak clearly enough," she said to Salem. Sabrina held the GPS closer to her mouth. "North Pole!"

A slight breeze kicked up, blowing sand around them, but they weren't transported anywhere.

"We just used up two guesses," she said, horrified.

"What do you mean 'we'?" Salem said. "I don't remember saying anything."

She glared at him.

He quickly jumped back to her side by saying, "The answer had to be the North Pole."

"It is," she said. "But that's the problem. There are a bunch of different North Poles." Sabrina thought back to her studies from the previous night. "There's the Instantaneous North Pole, the North Pole of Balance, the North Magnetic—"

"Sometimes you're just too smart for your own good," Salem interrupted her before she could complete the list. "Let's look at the clue again."

Sabrina thought back to what the camel had said. Checking down at the GPS screen she saw what it had recorded. It didn't take long for her to realize her mistake.

Where lines converge.

"It means the North Geographic—"

Zip!

"Pole," Sabrina finished in the frigid north.

It was freezing, or below freezing, to be more precise. Sabrina threw on her coat, hat, and gloves and gave them a little extra magical insulation, along with a pair of long underwear beneath it all. Assuming Salem was probably cold as well, she zapped him up a formfitting little snowsuit.

"Snazzy," he replied, strutting around in the suit.

Even though the sun was shining, it did little to warm the frigid air. Of course, being a witch, she could use her powers to warm her body, which she did for herself and Salem as well. Now, no matter what the external temperature dropped to, they would be comfortable.

Sabrina checked the GPS and discovered that they were much farther from the North Pole than they had been from any of their other destinations. *But it's so cool to be on top of the world,* she thought with glee. *Literally.*

She examined the area, knowing they were certainly safe from running into other people. The frozen tundra wasn't exactly hopping with tourists.

"If we're going to collect a splash of cold water," Sabrina said, "we're going to need another mode of transportation."

"How about a speedy snowmobile?" Salem suggested, practically panting.

"Sorry Salem," she replied. "I don't want to risk running out of gas again. It's too dangerous in this frigid place. I actually had something else in mind."

"Such as?"

"Well, it's something I'm going to need your help with," she said.

"Do I get to drive?"

"Absolutely," she said. "In fact, you're going to be totally in charge."

"It's about time."

Sabrina smiled. With a point of her finger she whipped up a dogsled with several growling canines in the lead.

Salem immediately jumped into her arms. "What are you thinking?!" he yelled.

"I need you to give them commands," she whispered into his ear so the dogs wouldn't come under her sleeping spell. "Tell them where to go."

The smile on Salem's face stretched wider than she had ever seen it before. "You want me to tell the dogs what to do?" he asked. "I'm going to love this."

Not wanting to risk speaking, Sabrina just pointed at him threateningly.

"Oh, like that's really going to scare me once we get into the no-magic zone," he said, hopping down from her and onto a perch on the sled. "Okay, listen up, puppies!" he practically barked at them. "We've got some distance to cover!"

Sabrina stepped onto the sled behind him, already regretting her decision.

"Mush mutts!" Salem yelled, and the dogs were off. "Mush!"

Since all Sabrina could do was hold on, she took a moment to rest as the sled sped along over ice and snow. She had been in a state of almost constant motion since she'd gotten home from taking her test that morning, and this was the first real break she'd had. Add to that the fact that she hadn't slept in over a day and a half and she had a feeling that exhaustion was starting to creep up on her. The only problem was that it was creeping up a little too quickly.

Sabrina felt her head drop down as she started to drift off into sleep. She quickly pulled her head back up and focused on the road ahead of them. *I think I need that splash of water for myself as much as I need it for the potion,* she thought.

Trying to focus on something other than sleep, Sabrina noticed they were making pretty good time on the sled. The GPS screen showed they were moving across the map and getting closer to the much needed potion ingredient. She couldn't help but wonder how many ingredients they would have to collect before they could start making the potion. She had forgotten to ask Prince Charming how many ingredients she needed, but she blamed her oversight on being distracted by his incredibly handsome face and sparkling personality.

Now that I think of it, Prince Charming never said what would happen if I fell asleep while trying to make the potion, she realized with a fright. But Salem's hollering distracted her from that thought.

"Move it, you mangy mutts!" he yelled. "I've seen turtles that move faster than you!"

Sabrina knew that the dogs probably couldn't

understand what Salem was saying, but she couldn't help but think letting him act so mean to them was a mistake. "Salem, knock it off," she whispered.

"Sabrina, you have to show these dumb dogs who's boss," he replied before turning back to the dog squad. "If only I had a whip! I'd make them move!"

The team of dogs immediately halted their forward progression. Contrary to what Sabrina had previously thought, the dogs obviously had understood Salem's threat.

"Did I say you could stop!?" Salem yelled with a deep voice. "We keep moving as long as *I* say we keep moving."

But Sabrina knew it was no use. The dogs were not going to budge. They were done taking commands from a mean cat.

Sabrina stepped off the sled, and her foot immediately fell into the snow and didn't stop falling until her leg had sunk down to the knee. She pulled it back up and shook off the snow. *I'm never going to be able to walk in this,* she thought. *Maybe I can send Salem ahead. He's certainly lighter than I am.* But Sabrina didn't want to risk letting him collect the ingredient in case she was supposed to do it herself.

"Snap to it, mutts!" Salem yelled in vein.

This gave her a deliciously evil idea. "I'm sorry, Salem," she whispered in his ear.

"Sorry about whaaaaat!?" he yelled as Sabrina gently threw him into a soft snowbank in the front of the dogs.

She could see the horror in Salem's eyes as he dug himself out and realized what Sabrina had just done. The dogs, however, seemed to be laughing—if dogs could laugh. Sabrina barely managed to grab on to the sled's front rail as they started up again, chasing Salem across the frozen tundra.

"I'll get you for this!" he yelled to Sabrina as he ran.

For a moment she felt bad for what she had done, but then, remembering how Salem had treated the dogs, she pushed past her guilt. She grabbed the reins to the dogs' harnesses, ready to pull them back in case they caught up with the cat.

The team was moving faster than they had before. The Salem bait had given them a renewed sense of purpose. Soon enough, Sabrina could see their destination getting much closer on the GPS screen.

"Hey doggies," she said with a sweet voice. "You've been a real help. Thank you." As they came up on a body of water, Sabrina gently tugged on the reins and slowed the pack. At first they fought against her, but were eventually overcome by sleep.

"Are you crazy!" Salem yelled, once the dogs were asleep. "What did I ever do to you?"

Like the burro and the buggy, the dogsled disappeared once it was no longer being used. The ice beneath Sabrina's feet was much more solid than the snow she had sunk into before. She could actually walk fairly well, as long as she managed not to slip.

Sabrina looked out at the lake. It was very large and looked rather treacherous. Ice chunks had broken off the edges and were floating across the surface crashing into one another. She didn't have to dip her hand into the water to know that it was freezing cold.

"Now what?" Salem asked.

Sabrina carefully stepped onto the edge of the ice and looked down into the lake. Deep below she could see something glowing. She looked back to Salem.

"Oh, no," Salem said, reading her mind. "I'm not going in there. I just ran a marathon with a team of dogs literally on my tail. It's your turn to do the hard work."

Sabrina knew he was right. She had already put

him through enough for the time being. Besides, she could really use the splash of cold water. She suspected that the spell she had previously cast to keep her warm would work under water as well. Removing her glove, she dipped a hand into the frigid water. It felt cold to her, but not bitterly so. "If I don't come up in a minute," Sabrina said, kicking off her shoes, "I expect you to come in after me."

"See if you can find me something to eat while you're down there," Salem replied.

Sabrina shook her head in disbelief. She was about to take a dive into frigid water with only a warmth spell protecting her, and all Salem could worry about was his stomach. She ignored him, took a deep breath, and jumped into the lake.

The spell worked fine. The water didn't feel any colder to her than as if it were at the beach in early summer. Sabrina kicked her shoeless feet as she turned her body in the direction of the glow. She didn't have very deep to swim. Salem would be disappointed that she saw no signs of sea life at all.

As the glowing water got closer, Sabrina pulled out the little bag. Using an intricate maneuver she managed to open the bag, collect the water, and close the bag all in one motion. Since she didn't see any bubbles escape the bag, she assumed she had managed to collect the water without releasing any of the gongs.

Sabrina turned herself back in the direction of the sunlight above. She swam as quickly as she could because she was beginning to run out of breath. It was only a few moments before she had broken up to the surface.

"Sabrina, help!" Salem yelled from behind her.

She turned to see him floating away on a chunk of ice.

Chapter 11

Salem was getting farther and farther away. He would never be able to swim back on his own. Sabrina knew that she'd never be able to swim out to him, either. She got out of the water and tried to find some other means of rescue as she slipped her dry shoes back on her wet feet.

"Sabrina!" he called.

"What should I do?" she yelled back.

"Get me out of here!" he screamed as the ice chunk he was on floated closer and closer to another. The two pieces of ice were about to collide.

Sabrina realized that since she had collected the potion ingredient, she had completed this part of the quest. Taking a chance, she pointed to Salem. He disappeared just as the chunks of ice smashed into each other.

The cat reappeared by her side. "That was close," he said with relief.

"My magic's back," she said, and gave another magical zap to dry herself off.

"Great," Salem said. "Now can we get out of here?"

"We have to find the—" Sabrina started to say as she nearly stepped on some words written in the snow. "Never mind."

Sabrina and Salem looked over the latest clue.

> In a prison land,
> A rich history clings.
> You'll know you're there
> When the fat lady sings.
> Clue five will you seek,
> When you count the sheep.

"That doesn't rhyme!" Salem shouted. "Seek and sheep! We both risked our lives up here, and they can't even manage to reward us with a clue that rhymes!"

"Salem, I think we need to focus on the task at hand," Sabrina reminded him.

"I was just saying . . ."

"I know," Sabrina said, trying to calm the cat.

She knew he was trying to get over the fact that he could have gotten hurt out there.

"Obviously we have to go somewhere that has sheep," Salem said, moving past his own fears. He was looking at the poor rhyme at the end of the clue.

Sabrina's eyes lit up. "There was a question on my geography test. 'Which country is the largest breeder of sheep?'" she said as she remembered back to the exam. "It's Australia."

"Are you sure you got the answer right?" Salem asked the rude, yet totally logical question.

"Yes," Sabrina said as she pointed at the words in the snow. "And look here. It talks about 'a prison land.' Australia used to be a penal colony for the British."

"Don't I know it," Salem replied. "I tried to convince the Witches' Council to send me there instead of turning me into a cat."

"But Australia wasn't a penal colony anymore when you were caught."

"Yeah," Salem said with regret. "The Witches' Council figured that out too."

Sabrina looked back to the clue. "And this part about the fat lady singing must refer to the famous opera house in Sydney."

"I don't think they raise sheep in the city," Salem noted.

"It's probably just thrown in to help," Sabrina replied. "I won't mention Sydney."

"Time to go!" Salem said, excited to leave the frozen wasteland.

Sabrina held the GPS to her mouth. "Austra—"

Day became night around them. "—lia."

Although it was a cool Australian night, Sabrina was rather hot in the layers of clothing she had on. She hadn't expected it to be so mild, but then she remembered that since Australia was beneath the equator, it was currently summer, whereas in Westbrige it was still winter. Either way, both Westbridge and Australia were much warmer than the North Pole had been. She magically lightened her load of clothing, removed the snowsuit from Salem, and turned off the spell that had kept them both comfortably warm in the freezing climate.

Sabrina could see fairly well because a full moon lit the night. They were standing in the middle of a huge expanse of dry land and had been conveniently deposited by the side of a dirt road.

"The GPS says that it's just after four thirty in the morning," she said. "Tomorrow morning, to be specific."

"So what fun, yet totally fallible mode of transportation are we going to take this time?" Salem asked, since there were no sheep for as far as either of them could see across the flat land.

"How about a motor scooter?" Sabrina said with a point as she zapped up the little bike. "With a basket for you!"

Salem looked at the basket Sabrina had attached to the front of the scooter. It had a plastic flower in the center. He was annoyed by her tendency to put him in these types of carriers when she conjured up transportation. "Great. And why don't you put a pink bow on my head too." Before he even finished the sentence, he was wearing the bow.

"Don't you look cute?" Sabrina asked in a babylike voice.

Salem ripped the bow from his head. "Does this thing have enough gas?"

"Looks like it," Sabrina said as she checked the gauge while hopping onto the scooter. "Come on, let's get a move on."

Salem reluctantly jumped into the flowered basket without a word as Sabrina tied the GPS to the handlebar in front of her. As she started the engine, she cast a little spell to make the soft motor even more quiet. She didn't want any loud noises announcing their arrival if she was going to have to sneak onto someone's farm. After zapping a helmet onto her head—and a tiny one for Salem too—she started down the road on the silent scooter.

Sabrina found the ride to be surprisingly boring as she continued along the dirt road. The ground was pretty even, so she didn't even have bumps or potholes to make things more interesting. She could only hear the whistle of the breeze blowing past her ears as she made her way. Even Salem seemed to be lulled by the ride as he chose not to speak as well.

Sabrina noticed that they were approaching the coordinates on the GPS. She was surprised that it looked like the scooter was going to take them directly to the sheep. This was the first vehicle she had popped up that actually made it all the way to their destination without stopping in the middle for one reason or another.

Sabrina lifted her eyes back to the road. It continued to drone on beneath her as the scooter's wheels rolled along the smooth dirt. Her jump into the cold water had sufficiently revived her, but now she was beginning to feel the effects of sleep again. The rolling tires made for a relaxing ride as she noticed Salem had laid his head comfortably against the back of the basket. The mesmerizing road was so calmly entrancing that she nearly passed the collection of sheep.

Dirt kicked up in all directions as Sabrina slammed on the brakes. Salem slid forward in the basket, his face pressed up against the side.

"Sorry," she said as he glared back at her. "We're here."

Sabrina coasted the scooter to the side of the road. She took Salem out of the basket and climbed off the bike. As soon as both her feet were on the ground, the motor scooter disappeared.

"I assume that means we're in the right place," Salem said, regarding the vanishing vehicle.

"Looks that way." Sabrina checked the GPS screen to confirm their suspicions. "Pretty convenient that these things keep disappearing when we're done with them. I wish my regular spells would be so helpful in cleaning up after themselves."

"Well, if we don't collect the potion ingredients, I guess you won't have to worry about messy spells ever again."

"Always looking at the bright side," she said sarcastically as another yawn escaped her mouth.

Sabrina walked over to the wire fence she had parked the now missing scooter beside. There was a large collection of sheep on the other side.

Sabrina could tell that there were at least three dozen of them in the field. Some appeared to be sleeping, and a few were up grazing on the grass. The land seemed to stretch on for miles, as Sabrina could barely make out the farmhouse that way off in the distance.

Although the sheep weren't really penned in, the entire flock had congregated in one area several yards away from the part of the fence where Sabrina stood. "According to the clue, we just have to count them," she said.

"And then what?" he asked. "Should we just speak the number into the bag?"

As soon as the question was out of the cat's mouth, Sabrina could feel the GPS device changing in her hands. The screen was shrinking, and the speaker area was morphing as well. Buttons popped out of the metal, and Sabrina could see from the glowing screen that the buttons had numbers on them.

"Look at this," she said as she held the device for Salem to see. "I guess we just punch in the number and something will happen."

"Okay, this GPS thing is a map, a people transporter, a coffee bean and sand locator, a transcription machine, *and* a calculator," he said in awe. "I have *got* to get me one of these things.

It's better than a Swiss army knife."

"Let's go count some sheep," Sabrina said as she moved over to a wooden post and placed a foot on the wire fence tied to it. She pressed down on the wire, and it seemed to hold in place. Grabbing on to the post, she lifted her other foot to the next wire and raised herself up.

Still grasping the post, she raised one foot over the top wire of the fence and swung her body to the other side. She dropped down inside the yard, unaware of the fact that the bag sticking out of her back pocket had snagged onto the wire. It had been pulled out of her pocket and was hanging precariously from the fence.

Salem didn't see the bag either as he crawled under the fence and joined Sabrina. Together they walked through the field with Salem in the lead. Since the cat was built close to the ground, he kept an eye out so that Sabrina wouldn't step in anything that she wouldn't want to get stuck to her shoes.

"This is going to be easy," she said. "All we have to do is count some sleeping sheep."

The breeze kicked up around them, cooling their faces. It also managed to blow the dangling bag off the fence and, as the bag fell, it opened just slightly.

GONG!

Sabrina reached for her back pocket and felt that the bag was gone. Turning back in the direction she had come, she sprinted toward the fence. At first she couldn't see the bag because it blended in with the grass. The moonlight wasn't helping, as the shadows just added to the darkness. She was finally able to make out a patch of red in the grass and she dove for the bag, pulling it shut before any other sound could escape.

There are still two gongs left, she thought with a sigh of relief. I hope it's enough.

Then, she heard the sound of baaa-ing behind her. She turned to see that the sheep were now awake and ambling through the field.

☆

Chapter 12

☆

"This isn't good," Salem said as the sheep moved along the field together in a flock.

Sabrina carefully followed the sheep, trying not to scare them into running away from her. They had conveniently managed to keep themselves in a group, but Sabrina knew that she'd never be able to count them if they kept moving. "Why don't you herd the sheep to me?" she suggested. "And I'll count them one by one as they pass."

Salem did not respond. He just stared at her as if he was waiting for something.

"Or I could just talk them to sleep," she realized, "then count them while they're all in one place."

"Good plan."

Sabrina hurried to the flock with Salem on her heels.

Sheeeep!" she called to them in a singsongy voice. "Heeere, sheeep!"

The flock began to slow as a couple sheep dropped off into sleep. Sabrina continued along with them, trying to reach the head of the pack.

"That's riiight. Goooood sheep," she said softly as she walked among the flock. "Go back to sleeep."

"Why are you talking like that?" Salem asked as he caught up to her. "They're going to fall asleep no matter how you say the words."

"Just trying to make it easy on them," Sabrina said with a yawn as they reached the front sheep.

The entire flock was now out. She looked back as the sleeping sheep stretched out behind her. It was a surprise to see that they had traveled so far from the point she had started talking them to sleep.

"Salem, you go to the last sheep and count from there to the first one," she said. "I'll start here and go to the back. We'll compare numbers when we're done."

"Gotcha," he said as he scampered across the field.

Sabrina started with the lead sheep. She wasn't sure but she thought that he was snoring. *One, two, three,* she mentally counted as she made her way back through the flock.

. . . *Ten, eleven, twelve,* she continued with a yawn. *I have been up for almost a day and a half. This is crazy. How am I supposed to get all these* . . . Sabrina stopped in the middle of the field, realizing that she had lost count.

Heading back to the lead sheep, Sabrina started counting again, paying close attention to the numbers as she moved past the sheep. She passed Salem at number twenty. The two of them nodded hello, but kept focusing on the task at hand. Sabrina's eyes began to droop as the number of sheep went higher and higher. With each additional sheep, she got a bit more tired. *Now I finally understand why people count sheep to go to sleep,* she thought.

Yawning, she finally reached the end of the flock of sleeping sheep. With the count done, she hurried as quickly as her tired legs could carry her back to meet Salem in the middle of the herd.

"Forty-two," she said with another yawn.

"That's what I got," Salem confirmed, yawning as well.

"Please don't tell me you're getting tired too," Sabrina begged.

Salem's face confirmed her suspicion.

"But you got sleep last night," she said.

"Maybe somebody shouldn't have forced me to

run a race across the North Pole," he said bitterly. "Just out of curiosity, do we know what happens to the spell if you fall asleep?"

"I've been trying not to think of that," she admitted. The most likely response for Salem's question was that everyone who had come under her spell would probably never wake up again.

"Don't worry, Salem," she said firmly. "That's *not* going to happen."

She punched the number of sheep they had counted into the GPS and waited for something to happen. A small piece of paper started to feed out of a slit at the top of the device.

"It's a printer, too!" Salem noted excitedly.

"I guess I just put the printout in the bag," Sabrina said, coming to the only logical conclusion.

She tore the paper out of the machine and confirmed that the number forty-two was printed on the page. She took out the bag, careful not to let it open again. They were running out of gongs in there, and she still didn't know how much longer they would be on the hunt. Folding the paper into tiny pieces, she slipped it through the small opening in the bag, not even bothering to pull at the strings.

Once the paper was safely inside the bag, she

returned it to her pocket. Then the GPS spit out another piece of paper before morphing back to its original shape. The numbered buttons were gone. Sabrina lifted the paper, lighting it with the bright screen of the GPS.

For a lullaby
On a merry-go-round
It's time to try
To collect the sound.
For your final clue,
Slumberland's for you.

"Final clue!" she said excitedly. "Woo-hoo."

"And this one's the easiest of them all," Salem said.

Sabrina looked back at the paper. "Slumber-land? Why do I get the feeling that place is not listed in any of my geography notes?"

"It's an Other Realm amusement park devoted to sleep," Salem explained.

Sabrina searched her memory bank. "I've never heard of it."

"It's not really popular," Salem further explained. "Most people usually fall asleep right after paying the huge admission fee. That doesn't exactly en-courage repeat business except for witches who suffer from insomnia and have trouble falling asleep. Not to mention parents of babies and young children who won't stop crying."

Sabrina yawned. "If we're already getting tired, how are we going to manage to get the last clue without falling asleep ourselves?"

"Willpower?" Salem suggested.

"That coming from someone with the least amount of self-control that I know," Sabrina said ruefully.

"We're wasting time," Salem said, changing the subject.

Sabrina pulled the GPS from behind her. "Take us to Slumber—"

"—land," Sabrina completed the word while they stood outside the gates of the theme park.

It was night once again, although Sabrina suspected that it was always night in Slumberland. Salem was right about the place lacking in popularity. There were only a couple of people milling around the entrance instead of the huge lines Sabrina usually associated with amusement parks.

Sabrina stepped up to one of the many empty ticket booths. "How much does it cost to get in?" she asked.

"Weeellll," the man behind the counter said in

the slowest manner she had ever heard. "That . . . depends . . . on . . . the . . . package." He indicated to the sign above him with the pricing guide.

Sabrina read the sign and found out that she could get a pass for the day, week, or entire year. Since she doubted that she would ever be coming back to Slumberland, she decided on just the day pass, but was shocked when she saw the cost.

"They have *got* to be kidding," she said to Salem

The sign above her read:

DAY PASS

COST: ONE ADMISSION
ADMIT ANY SECRET YOU HAVE
ADMIT THE TRICK YOU PLAYED ON YOUR BOYFRIEND
ADMIT THE BETWEEN-MEALS SNACK YOU SNUCK
ADMIT THE SPELL YOU CAST ON THE WITCHES' COUNCIL

THE BIGGER THE SECRET, THE BETTER!

"I told you it was a huge admission fee," Salem replied.

"Yeah, but you never explained that the fee was that I had to make an actual admission," Sabrina replied. "Sometimes I hate how literal the Other Realm can be."

Sabrina looked to the ticket seller, who was obviously waiting for her to admit to some really big secret in her life so he could let her in. The only problem was the biggest secret she had was that she was a witch—and she really didn't think that would count as a "huge admission" in the Other Realm. After a few minutes of thinking, she finally came up with something. She stepped closer to the booth so the few other customers around her wouldn't hear.

"I could have studied for my geography test earlier in the week," she whispered to the ticket seller, "but I got hooked on watching an *I Love Lucy* marathon on TV."

"Wait a minute!" Salem yelled. "We've been put through all of this craziness because you couldn't pass up an evening of classic comedy?"

"Unless I'm mistaken," Sabrina said, "weren't you the one who had put the TV on in the first place and convinced me to sit down and watch with you?"

"I just love that crazy redhead," he said, trying to change the subject. "She always gets into the wildest situations. Kind of like someone else I know."

"Now it's your turn to make an admission," Sabrina said, "and it had better be huge."

Salem looked straight into the booth, took a deep breath and said, "Salem Saberhagen. I'm on file."

The guy in the booth turned to his computer and slowly typed Salem's name on the keyboard.

"You're on file?" Sabrina asked while the man continued the painfully slow process of inputting Salem's name.

"When the Witches' Council got me to admit to my plan to take over the world, they kept pushing until I admitted to everything I'd ever done," he explained. "They keep the list on the Witch Wide Web."

"I'd love to see that," Sabrina said. "It must be some list."

"Yeah," Salem lamented. "It's got everything from my failure to pay magic taxes to the time I cast a misguided spell and actually turned the moon into green cheese."

"That was some mistake," Sabrina said with a giggle.

"I know," he replied. "I was trying to make it mozzarella so I could have the biggest lasagna in the universe."

"You . . . sucked . . . your . . . thumb . . . until . . . you . . . were . . . one . . . hundre\d . . . and . . . forty . . . years . . . old?" the man in the booth asked.

"And then they gave me paws so I wouldn't have any thumbs!" Salem whined.

Sabrina gave him a comforting rub behind the ear.

"Two . . . tickets," the man said as he slipped a pair of coupons through the hole in the glass window. "Have . . . a . . . nice . . . time."

"Thanks," Sabrina said as she took the tickets and moved away from the booth before the guy could say anything else. His voice was enough to send her into a deep sleep.

The front gate stood only a few steps behind the ticket booth. It was designed as a tunnel going through a pile of the softest-looking pillows Sabrina had ever seen in her life. She and Salem stepped to the gate and handed their coupons to a woman dressed in pajamas. The ticket taker gave Sabrina a map of the park and yawned in place of some silly greeting that would have probably been said at a different kind of place.

Sabrina immediately opened the map to look for the merry-go-round as they stepped through the turnstile. The clue had been straightforward enough to tell her exactly where she was supposed to go. But, more importantly, it had also indicated that this was the last ingredient for her potion.

"I guess we won't need the GPS for this one," Sabrina said as she scanned the map. "It looks like we need to go to very back of the park. This shouldn't be too hard."

"I'm not so sure about that," Salem replied.

As they stepped out of the tunnel and into the park, Sabrina took her eyes off the map and saw what had made Salem doubt her comment. Dozens of patrons were spread out in front of her, asleep. They hadn't even made it past the gift shops.

☆

Chapter 13

☆

"This doesn't look good," Sabrina said as she and Salem looked over the sleeping people. Entire witch families were huddled together, as they apparently had dropped off to sleep at the same time. They hadn't even managed to get more than a few yards into the park.

Slumberland looked like any typical mortal theme park. The long road that ran between the gift shops was painted in a rainbow design as soft, fluffy clouds lined the street. Granted, in a mortal theme park the clouds would be made of cotton or plastic as opposed to the real clouds floating around, but the effect was still the same.

The air in the park seemed the perfect temperature and was the most comfortable atmosphere Sabrina had been in since she'd left Westbridge that morning. Giant pinwheels turned in the gently blowing breeze. Sabrina was quickly mesmerized by the rotating colors moving at a lazy speed.

Realizing the hypnotizing power of the pinwheels, Sabrina reluctantly tore her gaze away from them. "Look at the ground," she suggested to Salem.

"What?" he said as he roused himself as well.

"This place is designed to put us to sleep," Sabrina said. "If we only look at the ground we might have a chance. And it will ensure that we don't step on anyone."

Sabrina watched as her feet moved one in front of the other. Stepping over sleeping tourists, she made her way past the long row of gift shops. Every now and then she had to look up to make sure they didn't run into anything, and each time she did, something new fought to pull her attention.

One time she looked up to see some water dribbling down the side of a building. The soft trickling sound that she heard was dangerously peaceful. *This is probably the quietest theme park in existence,* she thought as she put her head back down and saw that Salem seemed to be nodding off as well. "Stay with me, Salem," she said. "We're in this together."

"But it's so quiet," he replied as he walked right through a low hanging cloud.

Once they were past the gift shops they reached a fork in the road at the Lazy River Ride. Again, the calming sound of the water was doing its best to lull them to sleep.

Sabrina checked the park map and confirmed that they needed to take a right at the ride and continue past the Bed Bounce. The drawing on the map showed that the Bed Bounce—much like the name implied—was a giant bed for bouncing on. But when Sabrina and Salem reached that particular ride they found that the few people who had made it that far were comfortably lying curled up in the fluffy bedding.

"Sabrina, can we stop for a minute?" Salem asked with a yawn. "My paws are pooped."

"We stop, we sleep," she simply replied with a yawn of her own. "Keep moving."

They continued to walk, but it was at a pace that was considerably slower than they had moved all day. Sabrina's legs felt like lead, and seemed to get heavier each time she lifted one to put it in front of the other. It wasn't long before she gave up on lifting her legs altogether and just started shuffling them forward. She felt bad for Salem, who had four legs to keep moving.

"Are we there yet?" he whined.

Sabrina could hear a song being played in the distance. It was a lullaby, and she assumed that it was the sound they were sent to collect. "We're getting closer," she said, trying to confirm with the map. Her eyesight was getting blurry, and she had to keep blinking to get herself to see straight. "Do you think you can make it?"

He mumbled something in response.

"What?"

"I said, I think so." He was straining to get the words out.

The air around them was growing thicker with moist clouds. It was hard to push on. It felt as if they were walking through a warm soothing bath that Sabrina just wanted to lie down in and let all of her cares drift away.

The lullaby song was getting louder, but its soothing notes were not helping the situation. The melodic music swam through her head as she moved past the slowest-moving roller coaster she had ever seen in her life. It was empty.

Just as Sabrina could see the merry-go-round off in the distance, the lullaby song stopped playing.

"That's not a good sign," Salem said about the music ending.

"Come on," Sabrina said with a renewed sense of purpose. She pushed through the heavy air as she hurried to the ride. She didn't know why the song had stopped playing, but she was determined to get it to start up again. When she saw that Salem was having a hard time keeping up, she took him into her arms and carried him.

They reached their goal moments later and saw that the merry-go-round had stopped. The part of the park they were in was entirely empty except for an employee in a glass booth, who looked rather surprised to see them.

"Can you start the merry-go-round?" Sabrina asked the ride attendant.

"Talk into the microphone." His voice came from a speaker above the booth. He pointed to a device on the other side.

Sabrina noticed for the first time that he was wearing some kind of headphones. She walked to the other side of the booth and stepped up to the microphone. "Why did the music stop?"

"It only plays when the ride is in motion for the one test I have to perform each day to make sure everything's working fine," he explained via the speaker. "I've never seen any guests make it this far into the park before."

"Would you mind testing it again?" Sabrina

said, grabbing for the bag in her pocket. "We need to hear the song." She saw that Salem's eyes were beginning to close, so she gave a little shake to wake him.

"I'm only allowed to test it once a day," he repeated. "However, if you want to go on the ride, I can start it up for you."

"I don't know," she said, looking over at the carousel horses. Just looking at the ride made her yawn.

Sabrina could see the excitement in the man's eyes. She figured he'd probably never gotten to start the ride for anyone before, since most people fell asleep before getting this far.

"Oh, come on," he nearly begged. "It's the only way to hear the song."

"I don't think we have a choice," Salem said.

"Okay, but just a short ride," Sabrina said into the microphone. "Just one verse of the song."

"Okay." The man snapped to attention, readying the controls in his booth. His face was beaming. "Thanks!"

Sabrina walked over to the merry-go-round and placed Salem securely on one of the wooden horses. Saddling up beside him, she readied the bag to collect the song. "We only have two gongs left from Big Ben," she said to Salem. "How are we going to keep the bag open long enough to collect the lullaby without letting them out?"

"Very carefully?" he suggested.

Some help you are, she thought. Sabrina knew she didn't have a choice. She had to collect the last ingredient.

Sabrina waved over to the man in the booth, signifying that they were ready to start the ride. As soon as she felt the horse she was on begin to rise, she opened the bag. The first note played, and Sabrina sang along as the horse slowly moved up and down: "'Rock a bye baby on the treetop. When the wind blows the cradle will rock.'"

GONG!

"'When the bough breaks the baby will fall. And down will come baby, cradle and all.'" Sabrina pulled the bag tightly shut. "I managed to save the last gong!" she said excitedly to Salem, knowing that they had all the ingredients.

But Salem did not answer.

She looked over to the horse beside her and found the cat sleeping soundly. "Salem, get up," she pleaded, hopping off her horse.

But it was no use. He was fast asleep.

The attendant had shut down the ride as soon as the verse had ended, just like Sabrina had asked. Taking Salem into her arms again, she gave the ride attendant a wave of thanks before pulling the GPS off her belt.

"Home," she said into the device, and suddenly she was in the living room of her aunts' house.

Sabrina found her aunts sleeping in the same positions as she had left them. After putting Salem down on the couch beside Hilda, Sabrina moved into the dining room. She pressed on the control that activated Zelda's labtop, and the potion mixing station rose out of the center of the dining room table.

The GPS beeped, and she picked it up to see the instructions for mixing the Waking Spell potion on the display screen. Yawning, she also noticed that it was late afternoon. Her round-the-world trek had taken the better part of the day, and she was really feeling the effects of exhaustion.

Sabrina grabbed a beaker for mixing the potion. After wiping her bleary eyes, she opened the little bag full of ingredients that she and Salem had collected.

GONG!

The sole remaining gong spilled into the beaker, taking form as a bronze-colored liquid. She checked the GPS and saw that the next item to add was the coffee bean. Reaching her hand into the bag, she had to dig really deep inside to finally find the bean. At first she didn't even notice that half her arm had disappeared inside the bag that was hardly any bigger than her hand. She pulled her arm back out of the bag and dropped the bean into the beaker.

"I need a seat for this," she said out loud as she slid herself into one of the dining room chairs. Going back to the GPS screen, she scanned down the list of ingredients and saw that she just had to add them in the order in which they had been collected. *Seems easy enough,* she thought.

Yawning, Sabrina reached her arm back into the bag and found that the rest of the ingredients had mixed together into a thick paste of sand and ice water. She could also feel the slip of paper with the number forty-two written on it, but had no idea why the lullaby hadn't slipped out yet.

Fighting to keep her eyes open, Sabrina wondered how she was going to divide the mixed ingredients. Her mind slowly cleared long enough for her to remember that she had her powers back.

"Sand," she said with a point into the bag, and the sand jumped out into the beaker. The mixture lightened a little as it swirled in the glass. "Ice water," she added, add the clear water spilled out into the glass. *Must stay awake,* she thought, trying to will herself to keep her senses sharp.

Sabrina put her hand back into the bag and pulled out the piece of paper that she had recorded the number of sheep on. Her eyes were having so much trouble focusing that she couldn't even read the number. Carelessly, she dropped it into the beaker as the mixture swirled around it. A rainbow-colored puff of smoke escaped as the paper was absorbed into the liquid. *How pretty,* she thought as her head rolled to the side.

There was only one more ingredient left.

So tired. Maybe I'll just rest for a second, she thought as she laid her head down on the table.

The world around her went black as Sabrina fell asleep.

Chapter 14

The darkness began to lift for Sabrina as she slowly woke up. She could tell that there was light shining behind her closed eyes. Blinking them open, she saw that somehow she had managed to get up to her old bedroom. Light was coming in through the window, and when she finally adjusted to it she saw that her digital clock said it was nine A.M.

What happened to Harvey? she wondered, remembering back to when she had magically transported him into her bed before leaving on her global trek. *Was it all a dream?* Sabrina sat up in bed, stretching her arms. She felt fully rested for the first time in days. *If it was a dream, then why aren't I asleep in my own bed at school? Why am I at my aunts' house?*

And then a sudden fear overwhelmed her.

What if I fell asleep for twenty years, like Rip Van Winkle?!

Sabrina jumped out of her bed and ran out of the room. Heading down the front stairs, she noticed that her aunts and Salem were no longer sleeping on the couch. She wasn't sure if that was a good sign.

Sabrina hurried through the dining room and into the kitchen, where she found her family sitting around the table, having breakfast. *They don't look like they've aged twenty years,* she thought. *Then again, twenty years is nothing to six-hundred-year-old witches.*

"Good morning, sleepyhead," Zelda said from her seat.

"Did you have a good rest?" Hilda asked.

"Fine," Sabrina said, still wondering what was going on. "I had the strangest dream last night. You were in it and you were in it." She saw Salem on the counter, sipping from a bowl of milk. "And you were in it."

"It was no dream, dear," Zelda said as she zapped up a cup of tea for her niece.

"We really did see the world," Salem added. "And got it all in before dinner."

"But I didn't finish making the potion," Sabrina said, taking a seat at the table. "Did the lullaby spill out of the bag and get added on its own?"

"You mean this bag?" Hilda picked the familiar little sack off the table and handed it to Sabrina.

The young witch pulled against the drawstrings, and the lullaby popped out and hung in the air for a moment.

"Then how did we all wake up?" Sabrina asked once the song had finished playing. "And Aunt Hilda, you said the spell was easy to reverse. I don't consider running all over the globe to be an easy way to undo a spell."

"Actually, the potion you were making doesn't really have the power to do anything," Zelda explained.

"What do you mean, it doesn't do anything?" Sabrina asked in shock.

"Well, it does make a good car polish," Hilda added.

"Okay, I'm not totally awake yet," Sabrina said. "So please slowly explain what happened and try to use the simplest words possible. What was the easy way to reverse the sleeping spell?"

"All you had to do was fall asleep," Hilda said. "Once you went to bed, everyone you had knocked out would wake right up feeling totally rested and like nothing strange had ever happened to them."

"But what about the scavenger hunt around the world?" Sabrina asked. "All those things I collected by hand without being able to use my magic?"

"That was just to make you tired," Zelda explained. "In case the original spell you had cast was keeping you awake."

"So all that time I was fighting to stay awake to finish the potion," Sabrina said, "all I had to do was fall asleep and the spell would have been broken."

"Ironic, huh?" Salem said.

Sabrina took a few deep breaths to calm herself. "Why?"

"To teach you a lesson," Zelda explained. "This all started because you pushed off your studies until you had to rely on magic to avoid sleep. And as I said before, sleep is important. You shouldn't go messing around with your sleep cycle, even if all it takes is one easy spell in the Magic Book. Therefore, to reverse the spell, you were put through a series of tests where you couldn't rely entirely on magic."

"Now, don't you feel better knowing that you can do things on your own the mortal way?" Hilda added.

Sabrina knew that the lesson had been a good

one, but she still wasn't awake enough to accept that everything she had been put through was solely for her benefit.

"Why does the Witches' Council put these trick spells in the Magic Book in the first place if witches aren't supposed to cast them?" Sabrina asked the question that had been bugging her for years.

"How else are you going to learn?" Hilda replied.

"It's not like you ever listen to your aunts," Zelda added.

"So everyone I put to sleep is okay?" Sabrina asked, trying to move past Zelda's last comment.

"The mortals woke up feeling refreshed, and just assumed they had been so tired that they'd just fallen asleep right where they were," Hilda explained. "No one's the wiser."

"And Harvey?" she asked.

"We filled him in on everything yesterday," Hilda explained. "Then sent him home."

"Looking as confused as he usually does," Salem added.

"He would like you to call him, though," Zelda said, ignoring the cat.

Sabrina sat for a moment, sipping her tea. Once again, magic had caused more problems than it had solved. She wondered if she was ever going to figure out the proper way to use it. *Maybe that's why witches live so long,* she thought. *It takes a few hundred years to start getting the spells right.*

"Well, I'd better get going," she said as she got up from her chair.

"Since you're here," Zelda said, "why don't you stay for breakfast?"

"No, thanks," Sabrina replied. "I should get home to start studying for my finals."

"But you just finished taking your midterms," Hilda reminded her. "Finals are months away."

"Hey, there's no time like the present," Sabrina said. "Salem, do you want to come over and help me study?"

"No thanks," he replied, dropping from the counter. "I think I'm going to take a little nap."

About the Author

Paul Ruditis is also the author of two other *Sabrina, the Teenage Witch* books: #37, *Witch Way Did She Go?* and #43, *Topsy-Turvy*. He has written and contributed to several books based on such notable TV shows as *Buffy the Vampire Slayer, Enterprise, Roswell,* and *The West Wing.*

Have you read all of the books
in the Harvey Angell trilogy?

Harvey Angell brightens up orphan Henry's life like a supercharged thunderbolt, and nothing will ever be the same again! But Harvey Angell's true identity is a mystery—one that Henry's got to solve!

While on a seaside vacation Henry discovers the ghost of an unhappy girl haunting his rental house. None of the lodgers is going to get any sleep until Henry and Harvey uncover the shocking secrets of Sibbald House.

Henry finds an extraordinary baby hidden in his garden—a baby with tiny antennae instead of eyebrows, and ears that look like buttercups! Henry's running out of time, and he has to find Harvey Angell before this mystery turns into a cosmic disaster.

. . . A GIRL BORN
WITHOUT THE FEAR GENE

FEARLESS™

A SERIES BY
FRANCINE PASCAL

FROM SIMON PULSE
PUBLISHED BY SIMON & SCHUSTER

3029